Published by Bethany House Publishers
A Ministry of Bethany Fellowship, Inc.
11300 Hampshire Avenue South
Minneapolis, Minnesota 55438
ISBN:0-7642-2076-4
Printed in the United States of America.

Books by Beverly Lewis

The Sunroom

THE HERITAGE OF LANCASTER COUNTY
The Shunning
The Confession
The Reckoning

*This book is dedicated
to
the glory of God.*

*To every thing there is a season,
and a time to every purpose
under the heaven:
A time to be born, and a time to die....
A time to weep, and a time to laugh.*

—*Ecclesiastes 3:1, 2, 4* (KJV)

Reflections

I've spent a lot of time perusing old scrapbooks and childhood diaries of late. The notion that I am coming into my contemplative years is entirely settling, really. Like a warm hug from someone who loves me.

Perhaps this is why I find myself asking directions of a pediatric nurse on the third floor of the Lancaster General Hospital. "It's the sunroom I'm after," I tell her, noting the quizzical look on her young face. "I've come two thousand miles to see it again."

"The sunroom is being renovated...painted and whatnot," she says, pointing toward the southeast corridor. "Down there, beyond the roped-off area."

The nostalgic side of me feels the need to explain. "I'm writing a family history...including a section on my mother's illness. She spent many days in this hospital back in the early fifties."

I hesitate, wondering. Dare I share the whole story? I've heard it said that if a writer speaks the intended words—shares them verbally prior to the actual writing—it upsets the creative process. Assuming that to be true, I suppress my thoughts.

"Good luck," says the nurse, offering a smile. "And watch for wet paint."

I thank her and head down the hallway, accompanied by Aunt Audrey, Mother's youngest sister. We stand outside for a moment, peering in. "Is this how you remember it?" she asks.

It is. And I make a mental note to reread, as soon as possible, the numerous entries in my old diary describing my first visit here.

Casting a furtive glance down the hall, I proceed to lift the rope and step inside. "Mother used to call me from this room," I hear myself saying. "Sometimes I would play the piano for her over the phone. The music cheered her—made a difference, she told me."

I sigh, remembering the bleak, worry-filled days.

My aunt nods, her own memories filling up the silence.

I move closer to the windows, staring out at the altered skyline. So much has changed since my growing-up years here in this historic city.

My eyes roam across familiar sights—brick row houses, their front stoops and cement steps paving the way to cobblestone sidewalks just a few feet from busy, narrow streets. And stately trees—what abundant varieties—creating a canopy over residential side streets that eventually lead to Penn Square, complete with its white granite 1870s monument to sailors and soldiers, the ornate Watt & Shand building, and Central Market—a gathering place for farmers and merchants since the early 1700s.

In full view is the hospital parking lot, three stories below. "The nurses used to help Mother stand up at these windows so she could wave to my sister and me," I remark to my aunt. "Emily and I simply had to see with our own eyes if Mother was still alive."

How fresh, how terribly raw the girlhood recollection. Weeks on end, missing Mommy; wondering if she'd ever be well enough to come home.

Standing here in this place, gazing through the same sun-filled windows as Mother had, I recall the old feelings, the panic-stricken awareness that my mother had only six months to live, yet not knowing how to make the minutes stop ticking. How to keep her alive.

The actual sequence of events is somewhat vague, like a vast watercolor painting of a distant panorama. My life is filled up with my own family now—my husband, our children, and the activities of our lives. Yet the past beckons me; my mind wanders, and I long to walk the streets of my childhood, talk to the people who remember how things used to be. This is the reason I have come to celebrate a milestone birthday in Pennsylvania Amish country, to research the bygone days, to recapture more than mere details.

With the aid of my juvenile diary, I wish to sort through tender emotions and get it all down in writing for posterity. And for myself.

Whatever the truth about those long-ago days, it is a young girl's path to the heart of the Father—my soul's search for hope—that I will treasure most.

Chapter 1

When I was twelve, I made a naïve, yet desperate pact with God to keep my ailing mother alive. It was the first time I'd ventured something so brazen—making a contract with the Almighty.

Not a soul knew of it, not even my best friend, Lee Anne Harris, and certainly not my mother. Had either one of them known, my face would've stained red with embarrassment, because as bold as I had been with God, the opposite was true of my personality.

I, Rebekah Mary Owens, was born shy but determined, the first child of a pioneer minister and his wife, on an Easter Sunday morning in the southern end of the Susquehanna Valley, commonly known as Lancaster County.

Early on, I displayed a keen interest in the piano, creating my first melody at age four, followed by piano lessons under the tutelage of my musical mother. Prior to these events came my earnest prayer for a baby sister, and nine months later, Emily Christine arrived.

The first indication that I was to be a tenacious child was discovered by my mother as I practiced for a kindergarten recital. Again and again, my tiny hands performed the melody. Spellbound, I was lost in the simple beginner's song.

Then to my surprise, the stove timer began to *ding* repeatedly. "Time's up," Mommy called from the kitchen. "You've practiced long enough."

I slid off the bench and voiced my complaint. "Do I have to stop *already*?"

"It's suppertime, Becky." Mommy dried her hands on her ruffled apron, blue eyes smiling. "You do love the piano, don't you, dear?"

"Can we make the timer go longer tomorrow?" I asked, marching off to wash my hands.

Along with my passion for music came an equally strong affection for classic children's literature, followed by an emerging love for letter-writing. Soon after fourth grade, I linked up with a Canadian pen pal, and she and I attempted to outdo each other in the penning of epistle-size letters.

Next came short story fever, beginning in sixth grade when the teacher taught us to use quotation marks correctly. Delighted at the ability to make story characters "speak," my narratives became longer, novella-length works, assessed for literary quality by my dear cousin and friend Joanna. I made Joanna my captive once, reading her a seventy-seven-page story entitled *She Shall Have Music*.

It is not clear to me, however, when the fears first began. Perhaps they started when a school friend excluded me from her birthday party. No brightly colored invitation ever arrived in *our* mailbox, though I waited and hoped.

Might've been a simple oversight; maybe not. Still, I worried too much about it, despising the left-out feeling.

Shortly after that, I began writing in a secret diary. The diary lay nestled safely inside a lovely wooden case with a gold lock and key. There I recorded the disappointments of my young life—some more critical than others, including the entire year I had to exist without piano lessons. After we moved to the country, Daddy could no longer afford them, yet I continued to practice with a passion.

Not long after my diary-keeping began, Mother and I became even closer, creating delectable "Plain" recipes such as Gooey Shoo-Fly Pie and chicken and dumplings to surprise Daddy, working on sewing projects for Emily and me, and practicing piano duets. Sometimes Mommy sang and I would play the piano accompaniment. Oh, the glorious musical hours we spent together...my mother and I.

Then along about dusk, when the house was still, she'd talk to me about the Lord, trying to redirect my worries. She was usually pretty effective, too, because of her "hotline to heaven," as she called it. Through my grade-school years she often encouraged me to give my cares over to God, helping me memorize Bible verses...teaching me to trust.

My sister and I had contests to see who could recite an entire chapter from the New Testament by heart. We were doing just that the morning Mommy became ill with flu-like symptoms.

I wanted to stay home from school to be sure that she was all right, but Mommy urged me on. "I'll be fine," she insisted, even getting out of bed to pray a school-day blessing over Emily and me.

I wasn't interested in running the usual footrace

to the top of the hill that day, where school-age kids gathered to wait for the bus. Instead, I hung back, walking alone...talking to myself.

"What's that you're saying?" the neighbor boy teased.

"Nothing much."

"It ain't nothin'," he insisted. "I *heard* you talking."

I clammed up, shielding myself from the rude, prying world. Eventually, when I'd given the boy no satisfaction of an immediate reply—no hope for a future one, either—he scurried away to catch up with the others.

Days passed, and Mommy's "stomach flu" lingered.

I would remove my shoes before entering her bedroom, because the slightest jarring sensation caused her pain. It was becoming evident that something hideous was trying to choke the life out of my youthful, rosy-cheeked mother.

Once, I caught her sitting up in bed, staring at the dresser mirror across the room. "Do I look different?" she asked.

"What do you mean?" A lump flew into my throat.

"Do I look gray to you, honey?"

I surveyed her reflection in the mirror. My grandmother, her mother, had died of cancer when I was only five, yet I remembered clearly the ghastly pallor of her face.

"You're going to get well, Mommy," I said bravely.

Reclining against her pillow, she let the former question drop and posed another. "What did you do in school today?"

I sighed. "We had Choral Union, and the music teacher asked me to accompany the Christmas Ensemble." The class had been the high point of my day. "He picked me over all the other pianists."

"I'm not surprised." She smiled, her rosebud lips pressed together. "You have a God-given gift, you know."

Gingerly, I sat at the foot of her bed, wondering how close I should get. What if she had a contagious disease? What if I caught it, too?

I reached over and stroked the foot-shaped bump under the blanket. "I love you," I said, almost under my breath.

"I love you, too, Becky." She reached for her thin New Testament, worn with use. "I don't want you to worry about me." She turned the delicate pages to a passage she'd marked with a hankie. "I've been reading a wonderful Scripture this afternoon. Matthew four, verse four."

Eagerly I listened. Her smile, no matter how weak, encouraged me.

"It is written: 'Man does not live on bread alone, but on every word that comes from the mouth of God.'" She paused, closing the Testament. "I'm going to take that verse literally."

So my mother was going to "eat" God's Word by memorizing and reciting certain Scriptures. Daddy would be all for it.

But the weeks turned into one long month, and she grew weaker. She had to eat canned baby food because she couldn't digest regular meals. And she was too frail to walk the short distance to the bathroom, so Daddy carried her back and forth, casting reassuring glances at Emily and me when we poked our heads out of our bedroom. "Mommy's lighter than a feather," he'd say, which wasn't reassuring at all.

I would rather have heard that she was gaining weight, getting stronger. Feathers, after all, were for cowardly chickens and ancient great-grandmothers' beds....

That night I waited for the sounds in the house to fade. Then slowly, I tiptoed into my parents' room.

Daddy was snoring his usual repertoire with an occasional extra snuffle thrown in. Mommy, however, lay as still as can be, making no sounds at all.

In the glimmering moonlight, I knelt beside her, careful not to bump the bed. Quiet yet steady was her breathing, and I knew she was alive because of it.

I reached out to touch her shoulder-length hair, its gentle waves enticing me. But I hesitated, then cautiously touched her cheek, brushing my fingertips against the sweetest face in the world.

The melody from my new piano solo fluttered into my head, and I began to hum softly, oh, so softly. I remembered every piano recital, every single audition and festival of my entire life...because she had always been there, sharing the music with me.

I thought of God and His great wisdom, that He had given me a mother so much like myself, and I wondered why my heavenly Father would allow her to suffer so.

"Dear Lord, don't let Mommy die," I prayed. *"Please..."*

The music in my head and the prayer on my lips pushed against the black fear inside me and at last, at long last, my tears began to flow.

Chapter 2

Mommy was admitted to Lancaster General Hospital the next day, September sixteenth. I didn't have to memorize the date because I recorded it in my diary—along with my apprehension.

The next day the weather turned balmy, too hot for so late in the summer. Something was brewing. I could see it in the ominous gray bank of clouds looming over Jake Stoltzfus's barn to the north of us. I stared out the school bus window at the sky, wondering if the coming weather change was God's way of mourning Mommy's illness, too.

Several of my school friends thought I assigned too much importance to the intangible, insignificant things of life—cloud formations over Amish farm-land, for instance. So when I told Trudy Croft, who always sat with me on the bus, about my feelings— the way the sky looked and how it tied into my mood regarding my sick mother—she just stared at me. Like I'd flipped my lid.

"C'mon, Becky, do you *really* think the weather

has anything to do with that?" she asked, blinking her dark eyes.

"Maybe," I said in a whisper.

"Well, I don't. For one thing, the farmers want rain...so maybe God's answering their prayers."

Trudy had a point. Yet it comforted me to assume that the Creator of heaven and earth just might send along rain on a sobering, sad day—just because I missed my mother.

That afternoon, something horribly embarrassing happened during science class. Mr. Denlinger, whom I secretly adored, called on me to answer a question about amoebas. I was well prepared, had finished every bit of the homework the night before. But when I opened my mouth, I couldn't speak. My words—the answer to the science question—were trapped inside a huge, throbbing lump in my throat.

"Miss Owens?" The teacher got up from behind his desk.

I pointed to my throat as hot tears threatened to spill. Quickly, I looked down, dabbing awkwardly at my eyes while shuffling through blurred homework papers.

"Miss Owens, are you ill?"

I shook my head no, refusing to look up. It was my *mother* who was sick, but how could I tell him in front of my classmates? Seventh graders were supposed to be on their way to maturity, not sitting in class crying like a baby.

I simply couldn't reveal the true reason for my

silence. I'd be the laughingstock of Neffsville Junior High if I told my teacher how hopeless life seemed, how horrible my fears.

So to keep from receiving a low mark—or none at all—I hurried to Mr. Denlinger's desk. Opening my homework pages, I pointed to the correct answer.

He looked up and offered a most understanding nod, then miraculously, and quite discreetly, he handed me a hall pass. "Take as much time as you need, Becky," he whispered.

I'd never forget this moment as long as I lived. Instantly, the handsome, dark-haired science teacher rose ever higher in my estimation. But he was never to know the story behind the tear-streaked face or the muffled sobs in the hallway. At least not from me.

Chapter 3

As much as I wanted to visit Mommy, the hospital rules were strict: No visitors under the age of fifteen. Made no difference if you were family or not. Didn't even matter if you were your mother's over-anxious firstborn and hungry to size up the situation for herself. The policy stood, heartless and cruel.

"Why does it have to be that way?" I asked Daddy at supper.

"Because it is just assumed by the medical profession that children carry germs," he replied.

"But we aren't sick," Emily insisted.

"And *I'm* not a child." I picked up my knife to cut my meat.

Daddy, however, was lost in thought and didn't respond to my bold statement. No use trying to pierce through his private gloom on a night like this. Mommy was far removed from us—physically and in every other way.

Emily was first to notice that our kitten was

missing. Goldie, the older cat, was lapping up milk from a bowl in the corner of the kitchen. "Where's Angie?" my sister said, pushing away from the table in earnest, going to peer out the back door window. "Oh no! It's raining...hard!"

With that, I leaped up, too. Emily was right; the weather was turning bad, and rather quickly. The willow tree swayed back and forth like a dancer in slow motion, and the cornstalks in Daddy's vegetable garden rippled and shook.

"There's a weather change in the forecast. I heard it on the radio earlier," Daddy offered, getting up to join us at the window.

All of a sudden, I felt his arm around my shoulder, and when I looked, I saw that he was hugging Emily, too. The idea of the three of us encircled this way comforted me, unified us against the world.

"What'll happen to our kitty?" I mumbled. "She'll get soaked."

Without a word, Daddy headed for the coat closet. "I'll have a look outside." He donned his raincoat and hat and was out the door in a jiffy.

I pressed my hand against the rain-spattered windowpane, staring hard at my father's tall frame bowed against a bitter wind. He stepped off every inch of our rural property, including his beloved gardens, in search of the wayward kitten.

Slowing his pace, he scanned the long strawberry patch out near the split-rail fence that divided our land from the neighbors to the east.

"Where *is* she?" Emily said, standing sentinel at

the back door. "Why'd Angie have to go and run off?"

I wanted to say that the kitten was stupid, but the frustration I felt had far less to do with Angie's disappearance and more with Mommy's hospitalization. Rushing to the back door, I cupped my hands and called out, "Daddy, come inside! It's too cold to search."

Emily joined in. "Please, Daddy, come back!"

"You'll get sick, too," I shouted.

Like Mommy....

His deep voice responded, but not to our pleading. He was summoning the lost pet, again and again, amidst a now vicious storm—"Here, Angie-girl. Here, kitty-kitty"—till I was afraid the pelting rain might soak through his shoes.

Daddy had never cared two hoots about the cats. Goldie, the older feline, and Angie, the spoiled-rotten kitty, belonged solely to Emily and me. Occasionally, Mommy demonstrated a passing interest by feeding them scraps of food, especially leftover tuna. But never Daddy. He had more important things on his mind—studying Greek or Hebrew and preparing Sunday sermons—than to bond with stray mouse-catchers.

Tonight, however, Daddy seemed bent on locating our precious kitten, beating the bushes for her, while the first ice storm of the season pounded Lancaster County.

I made repeated requests for him to come inside and warm up, but determination, or something more, kept him outside.

His strange behavior frightened me. *He knows something about Mommy*, I thought, closing the door and shivering. *Something's terribly wrong with Mommy.*

At last, Daddy came trudging indoors, hair wet and face flushed.

"I wish you hadn't stayed out so long," I said, trying to hide my concern for Emily's sake. "Angie'll find her way back home on her own...won't she?"

"I certainly hope so." Daddy offered a brief smile. But it was the blank look in his hazel eyes that multiplied my fears.

"How was Mommy feeling today?" I blurted, unable to squash the question any longer and glad that Emily had busied herself elsewhere in the house.

He was slow to answer, removing his soggy shoes and placing them near the floor register before pulling out a chair. He sat down with a sigh. "Your mother is very ill, Becky. The doctors plan to operate."

His words, clearly stated, jolted my twelve-year-old heart.

I waited.

Surely there was more to it. Doctors didn't just perform surgery without a reason. They had to call the illness *something*. Mommy's sickness required a name. Like *measles* or *polio*....

I thought of Billy Thompson, the boy at our former school, stricken with polio. Billy's diagnosis had come just as we were packing up to move to the country. I remembered being terribly frightened about having lived in the same neighborhood with him, attending the same school. So when we left, I was truly relieved.

"Why do they want to operate?" I asked. "What's *wrong* with Mommy?"

"The doctors don't know" came the cautious reply. "That's why they want to perform surgery."

I wondered why her stomach had swollen up. "Maybe she's expecting a baby."

He didn't laugh, although he might've. After all, fathers were supposed to know these things. "No, honey, Mommy's not having a baby."

"Then what could it be?" I asked. "What's making her so sick?"

A flicker of a frown crossed his brow; it was obvious he didn't know how to proceed. I assumed it by the way his thumb and pointer finger slid down his jawline, bunching up the skin and coming to a stop at the point of his chin. He seemed stalled, groping for a comforting answer.

My heart sank with the silence. Knowing my father as I did, this hesitation only meant more fuel for worry.

"Daddy?" I whispered, my heart racing.

He was about to speak, about to offer a fatherly word—or so I hoped—when the doorbell rang. Both of us turned and looked toward the living room, somewhat awkwardly, I thought.

Emily flew into the kitchen. "It's Uncle Mel and Aunt Mimi!" she declared, her cheeks flushed with delight.

I sat still as Daddy went to the door to greet our Mennonite neighbors, Melvin and Miriam Landis.

We must've been very young when Mother started referring to our Plain friends as "Uncle" and "Auntie," because as they came into the kitchen and hugged my sister and me, then unloaded two bags of homegrown produce, I honestly couldn't remember a time when we'd called them anything else.

It was perfectly right for Mr. and Mrs. Landis to have been included in our extended family all these years. If ever I were to make a list of nonrelated friends, these cheerful folk would've been high at the top. There was something endearing about Aunt Mimi and Uncle Mel. Mommy always said it was the love of Jesus shining out of their German eyes. And I believed her.

After a bit of small talk, including the news that the kitten was missing, Daddy took our company's wraps and hung them in the coat closet, then led Uncle Mel and Aunt Mimi back into the living room.

Emily, full of questions, asked, "Can a kitten live through a downpour?"

"God gave cats and other animals survival instincts, darlin'," Aunt Mimi reassured her. "That means Angie will probably be all right."

"Thank you, Lord!" Emily exclaimed, running upstairs to draw her bath water.

Aunt Mimi chuckled a bit, then a more serious expression settled on her ruddy, round face.

I excused myself to wash supper dishes, hoping to catch an occasional phrase of the hushed adult conversation. Assuming that their talk was about Mommy, I prayed that one of them might come up with a solution as to what was making her sick. Something the doctors hadn't thought of, maybe.

Sudden scratching on the back door prompted me to drop the dishrag and rush to greet my drenched kitty. "Oh, Angie...baby, you're home!" I said, scooping her up in my arms and taking her into the living room.

Daddy gave a good-natured nod, but it was Aunt Mimi who jumped up and came out to the kitchen with me. "Now, ya know, the poor little thing oughtn't to warm up too awful fast," she said, her brown eyes shining.

"So I shouldn't just dump her in the dishwater?" I joked.

"Not on your life!" She laughed, and her jovial roundness seemed to shake all over.

Quickly, I located a clean terry cloth towel and wrapped the shivering kitten in it, wishing we had a fireplace.

"Some lukewarm milk would be real good for her." Aunt Mimi gestured toward the refrigerator, then removed a quart bottle of milk. "Heat it nice and slow, stirring it all the while," she said with a wink.

"Thank you." I appreciated her concern. It was entirely genuine, because I knew that Aunt Mimi was a cat person, too.

I found the smallest pan in the house and poured

in a tiny amount of milk before turning on the front left burner. Assuring her that the kitty and I would be fine, I turned my attention to playing nursemaid to my waterlogged pet, and our neighbor headed back to the living room.

Keeping my mind on the chore at hand wasn't easy, and I found myself tiptoeing across the kitchen every now and then, eavesdropping—kitty in tow. Daddy was doing most of the talking, though I couldn't make out every word. Occasionally, Aunt Mimi's voice came in short, choppy sentences.

Straining to hear, I held my breath. One word— timid and faltering—stood out above all the others.

Cancer.

My mother might have cancer!

The thought of it made me dizzy with dread. I wanted to burst into the room and confront my father, wanted to be told everything he knew.

But I wrung the dish towel hard, till it nearly twisted in two.

Chapter 4

After the neighbors said their good-byes, Daddy headed for his and Mommy's bedroom—probably to cocoon away from the world, from the bleak reality. But I didn't want him to shut *me* out. I wanted him to talk to me, treat me like the young woman I longed to be.

Hurrying to the old upright piano, I knew where I could find solace. The instrument had been in my mother's family for many years, yet it stood tall and elegant against the shortest wall—the wall between the living room and my parents' bedroom.

Although we didn't have many fine furnishings, we did have a well-tuned piano. To me, it was the prettiest piece in the house. Its dark wood gleamed, reflecting the light of the floor lamp next to it, drawing me to its familiar keys.

Shivering, not so much from physical cold—though I felt chilled just now—I lifted out the heavy bench and sat down. I thumbed through my repertoire book and began to warm up trembling fingers with a four-octave scale, first in A-flat major, then in the relative minor.

Mommy doesn't have cancer! I vowed, practicing the scales as if playing them fast might chase her illness away.

She'll come home soon. She has to come home!

I must've played the scales ten times, increasing the speed as I went, before turning to the *Impromptu* in A-flat by Franz Schubert—my Fall Festival piece.

Emily appeared in her bathrobe, blond hair wet and tousled in ringlets about her shoulders. She got down and crawled under the piano bench, whispering to the prodigal kitten who lay snuggled next to Goldie, the older, wiser pet. Remaining under the bench, she coddled them for a time, then got up and slid onto the bench next to me. She leaned against my arm, the dampness from her hair seeping through my sweater, but I kept playing.

"Aren't you tired of Schubert?" she said just as I finished.

I turned to face her, and she sat up straight, face serious, eyes pleading for an explanation. "If I don't keep working on this, I won't have it memorized and ready for competition," I said softly.

"Oh, you'll get the trophy easy," she said. "You *always* do."

I hugged her and shooed her off to dry her hair and curl it. Thankfully, Emily hadn't overheard the frightening word regarding Mommy's possible diagnosis. Whatever it took, I would shield my little sister from the awful truth. If possible, I'd take Mommy's place at home...for Emily's sake. Till our mother could return.

Hours later, I lay awake in bed, on the top bunk. I could hear Emily's steady breathing below me, and I leaned over the side to look at her. Poor little thing—stuck with a fear-ridden sister for a substitute mommy....

I shook off the notion, praying it would never be permanently so. Yet it was impossible to sleep. Worrisome voices filled my head, and soon it was Daddy's voice that began to drift up from the kitchen. He was talking to someone on the telephone. Probably Mommy.

Once again, I crept toward the source of the conversation—Daddy's end of it, at least. I sat at the top of the steps and caught snippets of information. Mommy's surgery was scheduled—for tomorrow!

Leaning my elbows on my knees, I listened, wishing I were older. If only I were fifteen, I could visit the hospital. Then I wouldn't feel so left out. Wouldn't feel so alone....

Downstairs, Daddy's chair skittered across the linoleum floor, and I dashed breathlessly to the bottom of the steps, peeking through the crack in the kitchen door. He'd hung up the black telephone, but his right hand was still resting on the receiver.

For a time, he just stood there, staring at it.

Then he sat down and leaned his head against the instrument, like a stone statue.

A thousand fears gripped my heart, and all at once I forgave my father for his aloofness...his preoccupation. He was clearly suffering—as much as I was!

I watched till I thought my heart might break. Turning, I took the stairs back up, two at a time, and slipped into bed without a sound.

Lying there in the stillness, I wanted to cry but couldn't. I thought of the saddest melody I'd ever played, but my eyes were stick dry. Sorrowfully, I bored a hole into the darkness as raindrops drummed on the roof.

Chapter 5

Ever since her kindergarten days, my sister had taken pride in her perfect school attendance. Perfect, except for absences due to blizzards and other inclement weather—things that couldn't be helped and didn't get counted against you anyway. Today, by all outward appearances, was to be an *imperfect* attendance day.

The cornfield across the road looked as if someone had draped a luminous silver-white sheet over its furrows. Yesterday's rain had turned to hard sleet—a freak September storm.

Along with the landscape, a layer of ice presented itself on the windshield of Daddy's old blue Chevy. I felt sorry for him, having to scrape off the miserable stuff on the day of Mommy's surgery. Yet I knew he would, because there was nothing—lousy weather included—that would keep my father from going to the hospital today.

Surprisingly, Daddy put his foot down about Emily and me trying to make it up the hill to the bus stop, even though my sister begged not to miss school. Daddy seemed terribly protective of us, and I knew why.

"Aunt Mimi will be over shortly," he said. "She'll make breakfast for you...spend the day."

"Growing girls need lots of fuel," Emily chanted, trying to hide her disappointment about not going to school. "That's what Aunt Mimi always says."

Then, after gathering us into the living room, Daddy read from the Bible and our family devotional book. He offered a prayer—longer than usual—for Mommy's healing and for divine guidance on the part of the doctors.

Again, I found myself holding my breath. He shouldn't say anything about the surgery or the possibility of cancer—not in front of Emily.

But he did. "Today...at eleven o'clock," he said, pushing up his glasses, "Mommy is scheduled for surgery."

Emily blinked silently, taking it all in. "Is she *that* sick?"

Daddy nodded slowly. "Many people are praying, people all around the world," he said, referring to our missionary relatives and friends. "God will take care of her."

Emily was sniffling. "You mean she's gonna die?"

I was pretty sure what my little sister was thinking. Lots of times when God "takes care of" a sick person, it means they just pass on to heaven where they are made well.

Daddy sighed, closing the Bible. "I didn't mean

to imply that Mommy would die. I'm trusting God to heal her."

Emily blew her nose, and I moved next to her and put my arm around her.

My mind was buzzing ahead. "Mommy can't die today—she's too young. Besides, we need her...*all* of us do." I almost blurted out that I'd feel lost in the world without my mother, but I ceased the barrage of words, helpless to slow my quivering heart.

Daddy got up and paced the length of the room. Finally, he stopped and looked right at me. "Becky, have you been praying lately?" He didn't wait for my reply. "Perhaps sometime today you might offer up your cares to the Lord."

I nodded submissively but felt sharply misunderstood. Daddy was doing his best to cope with an invisible weight, a burden yet unnamed. The worst part of it: I could only do so much to help him carry that load.

I was delighted to see Aunt Mimi arrive. She came, wearing high snow boots and a fur-lined parka, just as Daddy bundled up and went out to chip away at the ice on his car.

"Look, girls, the sun's trying to come out," she said. And we leaned into the window, looking at the eastern sky.

"Maybe it's a sign," I whispered.

Aunt Miriam set about cooking breakfast—

scrambled eggs and sausage, plenty of toast and jam, and hot cocoa for Emily and me. We watched as she made her favorite hot drink. First, she pushed the setting all the way up on the toaster because she planned to burn the toast. When gray smoke started billowing out of the toaster, we knew she was ready to scrape blackened bread crumbs into her cup.

Soon the teakettle was singing its whistle song, and she poured boiling water over the burnt specks in her coffee cup. The concoction was something akin to Postum, not coffee. But smelling it, I knew for sure she couldn't have paid me to take a sip!

Daddy came back inside while the car idled, warming up, and after some insistence on Aunt Mimi's part, he finished off a plate of eggs and sausage in nothing flat.

"See...you *were* hungry, Daddy," said Emily, grinning.

He made no comment but came around, kissing first my sister, then me on the forehead. "I'll call the minute Mommy's out of surgery."

I couldn't help noticing how smartly dressed he was, wearing his black pin-striped suit and dark tie—like he was going to preach a wedding. Or somebody's funeral.

We helped Aunt Mimi clean up the house after Daddy left, and later, the three of us made chocolate chip cookies—seven dozen.

While the cookies cooled, she read aloud from our old Bible storybook—her favorite kind of story.

Ours too. This time, God was asking Abraham to offer his only son as a sacrifice.

"Why did God want to test Abraham like that?" I asked in the middle of the story.

Aunt Mimi marked the book with her pointer finger, keeping it there as she explained. "The Lord wanted to give Abraham a chance to show his out-and-out obedience, no matter how difficult the divine request."

Instead of dwelling on the schoolwork I was missing, I thought about the Genesis story, though I'd heard it preached from my father's pulpit many times.

After lunch, I sneaked away to my parents' bedroom to write in my diary. The wind swirled outside, sending snow crystals tapping against the window-panes as I closed the door and curled up on Mommy's side of the bed.

Hospital rules may prevent me from visiting, I thought, *but they won't keep me from being close to Mommy this way.*

I pressed my nose deep into her pillow, breathing in the familiar scent of her hair, her perfume. And I remembered her face and her voice. My dear Mommy....

The multicolored afghan at the foot of the bed caught my eye, and I reached for it and cozied up in it. My mother had spent most of her free moments making this afghan last winter, taking time to teach me the single crochet pattern. My chain loops turned out floppier than hers, changing the rhythm of the particular row, yet she insisted on keeping them just as I'd crocheted them. *"Everyone has to begin somewhere,"* she'd said cheerfully.

At the time, I was struck with her amazing patience, her willingness to put up with my sloppy work when her own was meticulous and near perfect.

Now I found myself searching the entire afghan for those loose stitches. Locating them, I smiled, leaning back against the pillow. My mother didn't deserve to be suffering downtown in a hospital. She belonged here—healthy and energetic—with the family she adored.

Then allowing my thoughts to flow freely, unmeasured, I began to write:

Thursday, September 18

Dear Diary,

Someone I dearly love is in the hospital—my mother. I wish I could stop being so worried about her. I need more faith, I guess. Daddy says I should tell the Lord about it, but what he doesn't know is that I already have. Was I born a worrywart? Will I ever grow up, Lord?

Please, oh, please, watch over Mommy today while she's in the operating room. She's only thirty-five. Please, let her live much longer.

I'm trying to be brave, but it's awful hard.

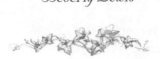

It was late when Daddy called us into the living room. We hadn't had a family meeting in several months, so it felt strange sitting there, just the three of us—without Mommy.

Daddy's eyes were sad, and slowly he went over the events of the day with us. "Mommy's surgery was exploratory," he said, then explained the word for Emily, even though he'd attempted to do so by phone earlier. "The doctors weren't able to remove the tumor. It's too widespread—" and here, he paused. Taking a deep breath, he went on. "They don't offer much hope."

Clenching my fists, I whispered to myself. "Not a tumor...not like Grandma."

Daddy must've heard me, for he worked his jaw silently, as if clenching his teeth. Emily began to cry, and he lifted my sister onto his knee. "I'm praying for a miracle. Remember, with God *all* things are possible."

I didn't doubt for a second that Daddy truly believed in divine healing. He preached it—had a strong faith. If God's Word said it, my preacher-father accepted it as fact.

Often he would "open the altars" on Sundays for people to come forward after the sermon. There sick folk were anointed with oil, and sometimes I'd seen them healed. Just like in the big tent crusades and revivals written up in the gospel magazines in

Daddy's office at church.

"We met with the surgeon today," he continued, "in the sunroom of the hospital."

"Why the sunroom?" It bothered me. Seemed too joyful a place for such a grim meeting.

"Well, it was certainly a private, *hopeful* place." He paused, adjusting his glasses. Then he went on to say that the sunroom overlooked the hospital parking lot and maybe, "when Mommy gets a bit stronger, the nurses could wheel her up close to the southeast window."

"So we can see her again?" I said, trying to still the terror gnawing at my heart.

Visualizing that scene in the sunroom was easy enough for a girl with a powerful imagination. Sunlight was surely streaming through the windows, tall plants scattered here and there. And the relatives—Mommy's father and stepmother and Aunt Audrey—they all would have been sitting with Daddy, waiting to hear the doctor's words.

"*We* should be allowed to visit Mommy, too," I fussed.

He pulled me over next to him. "Your mother's weak from the surgery. It's very important that we follow hospital rules."

"But if she's dying..."

"Please don't think that way, Becky," he reprimanded. "God's promises are sure. We must exercise faith for your mother's complete healing."

"Not everybody gets healed," I whispered, almost ashamed of myself. Was I a doubting Thomas?

This time I didn't wait for his answer. Turning, I clung to his neck. I wanted tomorrow to come quickly so I could wake up from this nightmarish dream.

Mommy couldn't die. Not now. I needed her, needed her more than ever. She understood me, knew me, loved me—her absolute, total worrywart.

My mother had a knack for offering encouragement when schoolmates misunderstood my passion for the piano, when some of them acted jealous because I consistently won at Piano Guild and other musical competitions. The repetitious practice of scales and finger techniques had never annoyed her. If anything, they brought her joy, because music was also dear to my mother's heart.

Then, too, there was my fascination with writing: diary accounts of special and not-so-special events, a spiritual journal, and the personal notebook where I recorded my most private thoughts and feelings. Some mothers might have scolded, feeling I'd taken my life's obsessions a bit too far, but not *my* mother. She knew me...through and through. And I couldn't imagine my life without her!

Chapter 6

I remember the first time I ever saw Daddy cry. It happened in church, the Sunday after Mommy's operation.

My father, leaning hard on his pulpit, began to ask the congregation to pray. "As most of you know, Mrs. Owens is desperately ill." In church, he always referred to Mommy as Mrs. Owens. "The doctors say that, aside from divine intervention, she has six months at the most."

He paused as if struggling to breathe. "I am asking...I *covet* your prayers for my wife." He slumped against the wooden podium, tears rolling down his thin face.

Shocked at this display of emotion, I stared in disbelief. My preacher-daddy had never allowed this weak, almost helpless side of him to spill out onto our church family. I felt limp as I witnessed my father's absolute humanity. Oh, now and then he'd let it show in the way he might surprise Mommy with a tender kiss or hug, but long before today I'd

set the Reverend Owens up on a high and lofty place in my mind—exalted him almost next to God the Father himself.

Of course, Daddy had no idea how I felt. If he had, he would've set me straight, but good. Yet I couldn't help it. My parents were my all in all, they and each of our friends and family at Glad Tidings Country Church.

Soon, Daddy's weeping made me cry, too. I wanted to run to him, comfort him up there on the hand-hewn platform, but I was too young and too shy.

Next to me, on the pew, Emily kept swinging her legs, irritating me. "Sit still," I whispered, putting on a frown.

Surprisingly, she stopped kicking, but only for a few seconds. Probably her little-girl way of dealing with the painful public announcement. The whole world—*our* world—had heard the news. Mommy was dying.

I prayed silently, pleading with God to heal Mommy and to help Daddy stand tall again.

Angie, our runaway kitten, was waiting for us after church as we pulled into the driveway. She was all curled up in a ball on the porch, soaking up the sunshine. Looking at her, I wished I could wrap myself up that way, tight and secure—sheltered from my pain. My dread.

After dinner, I went to my room and struggled

to express my feelings about the church service in my diary. Since Mommy's surgery, I found myself drawn to recording my thoughts every single day, either writing them down on paper or tucking them away in my mind for later. Today was no different.

Sunday, September 21

Dear Diary,

Today I tried to act grown up in church, but it was next to impossible. I fished, all teary-eyed, in my pocketbook for a hankie. Daddy was up there crying about Mommy, and I was doing my best to look brave for him. But it wasn't easy because something powerful was going on inside me, and I knew, just as sure as I love music and books and writing, that God in heaven wants me to do something. Something that might change the course of history—at least my history. Because there's no way I'm giving up and letting Mommy die....

I couldn't stop thinking about the Bible story, the account of Abraham offering up his son Isaac. It haunted me for days—played into my heart the way a soul-stirring melody grips a pianist's sensitive fingers.

If only summer were here, maybe then I could

deal with my life and its dire circumstances by playing softball with the neighborhood kids. It was one of the activities that helped ease my worries.

Actually, I played on an all-boy team, and I knew—secretly, of course—that they thought my being a tomboy made me a great player. But, sad to say, the tomboy thing was fading fast, and I fretted about the changes my body was beginning to make. Even more so now because Mommy wasn't around to help me through my transition to womanhood.

Before prayer meeting on Wednesday night, I mustered up the courage to ask if we could call the hospital. "I need to talk to Mommy," I said hesitantly.

Daddy stopped twisting the can opener. "Well, I hadn't thought of it, but..." He paused, leaving the soup can unopened.

"It won't take long. I promise."

An unexpected smile broke over his face. "It's a splendid idea." And he washed and dried his hands. "Emily can say a few words, too."

He dialed, and eventually a nurse must have put Mommy on the phone. My parents talked briefly, then it was my turn. But I froze up, could hardly think of what to say as I held the heavy receiver in my left hand.

"Hello, Becky." Mommy's gentle voice made me miss her even more. "I'm so glad you called."

"Me too," I mumbled.

"How's school? Still working on your Christmas program?"

"It's starting to sound pretty good," I managed. So much I wanted to say, but glancing around the kitchen at Daddy and Emily, I knew there was no hope of sharing my personal concerns this time.

"I've been singing," she said.

"You have?"

"Yes, with your auntie Audrey and one of the Christian nurses here. They come to tuck me in nearly every night."

"What songs?" I asked, eager to know.

"Oh, different hymns and praise songs...you know, the ones I love."

"Can't wait till you come home, Mommy." Her name stuck in my throat.

"Look up this Scripture tonight before you go to bed," she said. "Malachi chapter four, verse two."

Hopeful, I asked, "Is this a special verse from the Lord...just for you?"

I could hear her sigh, perhaps gathering strength. "All of God's Word is given to encourage and strengthen His children, honey."

"So it's *not* a direct message?" I queried.

She didn't say it was or it wasn't. "Jesus has been very near to me these past few days" was all she would confess.

"I'm glad He's with you," I said. "Wish I could be, too."

"I know you do, sweetie. Have Daddy call again, all right?"

Emily's turn. I had to say good-bye and I dreaded it. More than anything, I wanted to hold the phone in my hand forever. "Uh, Mommy? I'm going to write you a letter and send it along with Daddy tomorrow...okay?"

"I'll look forward to it, Becky. Remember, I love you." She sent a kiss twice into the phone, but when I tried to pucker, my lips trembled, and the kiss came out flat.

Chapter 7

I was the last one at the altar after prayer meeting. Lee Anne and I had started out praying together. We often knelt at the altar after church. It was part of the specialness of being Christian best friends.

Sometimes she'd have a request—maybe an important science project was coming up—and I'd agree in prayer with her for divine help. Other times, I'd bring a need, or we both would.

Up until tonight, I hadn't been able to put into words the burden weighing on me. Lee Anne surely knew what was bothering me—my mother's diagnosis—but she was more than kind that way and never pushed.

When she had to leave for home with her parents, I was still kneeling at the altar, scrunched down with my head buried in my hands. My heart cried out for mercy, but my mind was reeling with the story of Abraham and Isaac.

"Lord Jesus," I prayed, "one of these times, I want to make a bargain with You. I'm not sure how

You'll take it, but Mommy needs Your help getting over the cancer. And...maybe, Lord, You could use a little help, too. This is Becky Owens, Your faithful girl. Amen."

When I looked up, the sanctuary was dark. Someone, probably the janitor, had forgotten that I was still praying. It wasn't his fault, really. After all, I'd been awful quiet about it. Not like several of our church deacons, who sometimes got blessed and couldn't help raising their voices in worship to God.

I felt my way along the altar railing to the wall, then followed the dim light out to the foyer. There were voices coming from Daddy's office, and I stepped away from the door. Someone must be receiving pastoral counsel, so I slipped into the last pew of the shadowy sanctuary and discovered my little sister, curled up like a cat, sleeping.

Waiting for my eyes to grow accustomed to the dark, I closed them, praying for whoever was sitting in Daddy's office. My thoughts turned quickly to Mommy, who was hopefully asleep in her hospital bed.

My next conscious recollection was of being helped up the bunk bed ladder to my high perch, still wearing my mid-week church skirt and sweater. Seemed to me as if it was the middle of the night. The clock alarm on my dresser would be sounding early so I didn't mind sleeping in my clothes.

Hours later, Emily walked in her sleep. Either that, or she needed a drink of water and bumped into the bookcase on her way to get it. Anyway, because she hardly ever got up in the night, I tried to stay alert till she wandered back to bed. "You okay?" I asked when she'd settled into the lower bunk.

"Mm-m."

"You're sleepwalking, aren't you?"

No answer.

I peered over the side of my bunk, gazing down at her in the moonlight. Fully awake, I scooted to the ladder and hurried down, changed into my pajamas, then undressed my sister, pulling her flannel nightgown down over her limp head.

The next morning, she didn't remember being shuffled about by her big sister. I quizzed her repeatedly at breakfast, and she only laughed. Didn't believe me.

After the dishes were rinsed and stacked in the sink, I hurried back to my room to write the promised letter to Mommy. Much of what I had to say was personal, and I wondered if someone—one of the nurses or a doctor—might stumble upon my letter unintentionally. I couldn't risk having my private questions viewed by anyone other than my mother, so I decided not to divulge *everything* that was on my mind.

Thursday, September 25

Dearest Mommy,
     You sounded so happy on the phone last night, I could hardly believe you are

*sick at all. Everyone at church is praying
for you, and so am I.*

I couldn't tell her I was close to presenting a
proposition to God. She might not agree. My parents were never big on making deals with the Lord
or "putting out fleeces," like some folk we knew.

*The Schubert Impromptu (the one you
love) is completely memorized. My
teacher is pleased with the extra expression I'm putting in, especially the middle
section. You know, where the music
changes and it sounds minor—almost
like a thunderstorm, remember?*

*Oh, I almost forgot. I looked up the
verse in Malachi at church, and I love it!*

I didn't go on to tell her that I'd already memorized the King James version of it: "But unto you
that fear my name shall the Sun of righteousness
arise with healing in his wings."

My parents, of all people, revered the Lord's
name. It was the perfect verse to stand on, and I
did. Even told my sister about it as we walked
together to the bus stop.

"Do you think Jesus has wings?" she asked
halfway up the hill.

Good question.

"He might, now that He's in heaven, but I don't
think that's what the verse means. Wings are for

angels mostly, I think."

"Does it mean that Mommy's gonna get well?"

I had to be careful what I told her, because six months from now, Emily would hold me to whatever I said.

"Mommy's talking to Jesus a lot these days. Reading the Bible, too." I didn't say that our mother was too nauseated to eat on occasion, so she was devouring God's Word for her nourishment. "When you get really close to the Lord, sometimes He gives you promises, you know, from the Scriptures."

"But Mommy's been close to Jesus ever since she was little, right?"

"And she's *always* enjoyed reading the Bible," I added. "So we mustn't worry about her, okay?"

Emily nodded her head, eyes bright with hope. She listened as I explained that Mommy was having a medical procedure to kill off the cancer cells. "It's radiation treatment."

"Will it make her well again?" she asked.

"Hope so."

"Me too." She reached for my hand.

We'd come to the crest of the hill, where a group of seven or eight kids were waiting. When the bus came and we got on, I waved to Trudy Croft, giving her the high sign. She seemed to understand and slid over against the window. I squeezed Emily in between Trudy and me, right where a worried little sister oughta be.

During Home Ec., I made a mistake, though not over the measurement of an ingredient or something food-related. I let the word *cancer* slip out when I told my baking partner that my mother was in the hospital.

The girl who shared my work station immediately walked away and washed her hands, glancing anxiously over her shoulder. I wanted to tell her that the disease wasn't catching, that she didn't have to worry.

By the time I had Phys. Ed., everyone in track 7-Y—*my* class—knew about Mommy's hospitalization, that she had terminal cancer. I ended up taking a shower in the farthest stall, hoping to quell the apparent panic.

But nothing really helped. People didn't seem to understand about cancer—especially kids my age. No, I was the daughter of a contaminated woman. A frightened, rejected girl on the verge of puberty, who needed her mother more with each day that passed.

Chapter 8

When the phone rang, I had a feeling it was Mommy. I was right. She wanted to hear the Schubert piece, the one for Fall Festival.

Daddy pulled the telephone cord around the corner and into the living room, stretching it taut as he held the receiver in midair. "That's as far as it'll reach," he said, pointing it toward the piano across the room.

I scooted the bench out. "Think she'll be able to hear?"

"Play just the first two lines, okay?"

I placed my hands on the keys, and the melody began to ring out, softly at first. Taking care to voice the top notes, I leaned my right hand into each triad. Then I stopped at the appointed line and turned to Daddy, waiting as he talked to Mommy.

"How's that, hon?" Soon he was nodding his head, motioning for me to start again and play the solo straight through.

Happily, I performed it as if I were sitting at the

concert grand on the J. P. McCaskey High School stage. I thought of the music judges—how they would stop to write their comments, never once conferring with one another. But mostly I thought of Mommy and how she loved this piece.

When it came time for the final three chords, the *rubato* added the depth of drama I longed to express, perfectly timed.

Emily clapped loudly from the kitchen, and when I turned around, Daddy beamed his approval. He held up the phone. "Come talk to your mother."

"Hello?" I said, breathlessly, into the receiver.

"Oh, Becky, it's wonderful. You're playing it beautifully...you're really ready, aren't you?"

"The piece needs to settle down a bit," I replied. "But at least I have a good four weeks for that to happen."

"I hope you'll play it at school or try it out on some friends before competition," she said.

"Well, you know how it is at school...."

"You have a sweet spirit about this talent of yours, Becky. Don't let anyone discourage you."

I sighed. "It's just that my school friends don't understand why I need to practice so much. Trudy especially. And Suzanne and Doris both think I'm weird."

"But they play field hockey and run track all hours before and after school and don't think a thing of it, do they?"

"With music it's different. If you're not in the school marching band, you're just not that great," I said, anxious to hear how she was feeling, yet too nervous to ask.

"Well, always remember this: I think you're far better than simply great, honey, so keep up the good work, okay?"

"Thanks," I murmured and started to hand the phone back to Daddy. But she was still talking. "The letter you wrote was so sweet, Becky. Daddy brought it to me this morning as I sat in the sunroom, praying. I've read it at least three times."

"I'll write again," I said, stealing a glance at Daddy and Emily. "Maybe some girl stuff, next time."

"I understand," she said quietly. "Good-bye, dear."

"Bye, Mommy."

Daddy was interested in talking to her more privately. He went into the kitchen and turned off the light, so Emily and I headed upstairs for bed.

"We're going to Aunt Mimi's house this weekend," my sister said as we undressed.

"How do you know?"

She tossed her knee-highs on the floor. "I heard Daddy calling Uncle Mel before supper...in his bedroom."

"Not *his* bedroom," I shot back. "It's still Mommy's room, too."

"Well, you know." She glared at me. "Do you wanna hear the rest or not?"

I folded my arms and stood in the doorway. "What's to hear? We're being sent away again."

"How can you say that?"

"Well, it's true, isn't it?" I felt instantly lousy for letting such words slip out.

"Daddy can't handle everything, you...me...his sermons. Plus all the hours at the hospital." Emily sounded surprisingly grown-up for just having turned nine. Was this the same girl who'd asked me today about the Son of God sprouting wings?

"I don't mind going to Uncle Mel and Aunt Mimi's," I spoke up.

"Me neither," she replied.

"We're family there."

Emily started to giggle. "Aunt Mimi sleeps with her glasses on."

"Are you sure?"

She nodded, her blond curls dancing about her shoulders. "I saw her once when she was taking a nap. She says, 'A person's gotta see what she's wakin' up to.'"

"Oh well, naps are a different story," I said. "Betcha she doesn't wear them to bed at night."

"Guess we'll find out, won't we?"

"Guess so." I picked up Emily's socks and tossed them into the hamper without scolding her.

After we said our prayers, I waited for Emily to slip into bed before I turned off the dresser lamp. I felt my way through the darkness, careful not to trip on anything and break my arm...or my fingers, what with a piano competition coming up. I'd heard once that a famous musician had insured his hands for a million dollars each, and thinking about it now, I wondered if playing the piano was his only means of earning money. Or maybe he simply loved the feel of the keys beneath his fingers, the sound of the instrument. Probably both, I decided.

After slipping into my bed, I slid my right arm down along the wall side of the bunk beds and whispered to Emily. "Sorry about acting so sassy."

I felt her warm hand grasp mine and hold on. "I forgive you, Becky. Will you forgive me?" she said, almost sheepishly.

I said yes and fell asleep lying on my stomach, my arm draped down between the bed and the wall, holding the small hand of my only sibling.

That night I dreamed that Mommy was at home, weeding Daddy's garden, humming up a storm—never had had cancer at all. It was summer, and we were planning a family vacation to the beach. Emily had taken my spot on the boys' softball team, though, and I was livid. Because of it, I played the piano nonstop for days, working out my frustration.

I awoke with a start, my arm completely numb. Pulling myself together, I rolled onto my back, experiencing the electric tingles that come when the blood begins to flow freely again.

As I waited for the annoying sensation to subside, I thought of my prayer at the altar last night and the promise of a pact. The Lord would be waiting. What could I possibly do to move the hand of almighty God? Should I pray longer? Go without eating?

I contemplated to the point of frustration. Should I find a special sequence of words or phrases?

Write out my prayers so they were perfect? What?

Maybe begging and pleading would help. Maybe then God would heal Mommy. But...my heavenly Father already knew how badly Emily and I wanted our mother to be healthy again. None of my ideas were right.

Tomorrow, and not a day later, I will work this out and present it to God, I decided.

In my haziness, I felt absolute joy.

Chapter 9

Friday after school, before Daddy took us to the neighbors' house for the weekend, I asked if I could speak to Mommy on the phone privately, feeling the warmth creep into my neck.

Daddy, looking equally embarrassed, nodded and left the kitchen. Thankfully, my sister was upstairs doing her last-minute packing—sets of paper dolls: some cut out; others brand-new.

The phone number was written in my father's bold hand on an index card and posted with tape to the cover of the telephone book. I dialed quickly, hoping I could go through with this much-needed conversation.

It turned out that Mommy had been wheeled down to the end of the hall, where she was enjoying the sunroom. "I'll have her call you from there," said the cordial nurse.

"Thank you." I hung up, thinking of Mommy's special place, how she'd described the flowering plants, the window seat filled with pillows...the brilliant, soothing sunlight.

By the time she returned my call, Emily and Daddy were standing by the doorway, itching to load up the car.

"Go ahead," I told them. "I'll talk fast."

Mommy was on the line. "Hello? A nurse said someone called from this number."

From this number? It was *her* number—from her own home! Had she forgotten so soon?

I swallowed hard and took a deep, deep breath. "This is you, isn't it, Mommy?" It didn't really sound like her. She sounded distracted, dazed.

"Where's your father?" she asked.

I turned to look out the back door window. "Uh...he's putting suitcases in the trunk. We're going to Uncle Mel and Aunt Mimi's for the weekend."

She was silent.

"Mommy?"

She exhaled into the phone, and I could almost feel the pain in her sigh. "Have a nice time. Mind your manners, please, and tell your sister to do the same."

"We'll behave," I promised.

She was coughing now, and the phone thumped, like she'd dropped it.

"Mommy, are you all right?" I waited, hoping the nurse might pick up the receiver and talk to me, let me know my mother hadn't fallen or worse. But no one came on the line, and I rushed outside to tell Daddy. "Hurry! Something's wrong!"

He dashed into the kitchen, picked up the phone and listened for a moment, then clicked the phone over and over. "There, that's it," he said at last. "I hear the dial tone."

"But Mommy didn't say 'good-bye,'" I insisted. "She never said it!"

Quickly, he dialed again. When he finally got through, it seemed as if the nurse was doing most of the talking. Daddy hung up much too quickly, then looked kindly at me. "Your mother hasn't fallen, Becky. She's all right."

"But, Daddy, I—"

"We must put our trust in the Lord, honey."

I followed him to the hall closet, still frightened as we grabbed our sweaters.

It had turned warm again, and a full-blown Indian summer was in the making. At least, that was the current weather condition and promised to be the outlook for the entire weekend.

"Maybe you girls can play in the hayloft at Uncle Mel's," Daddy said on the way. "Sounds like fun to me." He was attempting to divert my thoughts, I knew. Still, I was worried—even had developed an upset stomach over Mommy's odd behavior on the phone.

Emily interrupted my thoughts. "We *love* jumping out of the loft window, down into a big pile of hay. It's great fun!" she said.

I couldn't begin to think of enjoying myself at the Mennonite farm, not with Mommy so much worse. The sound of her pitiful voice echoed again and again in my head. A gnawing dread ate at me. She'd never said good-bye!

On top of everything else, the prayer-decision loomed in my mind and in my heart. Evening was fast approaching; I had to make up my mind about the deal. My pact with God.

Daddy switched radio stations, from the news to classical music. The glorious sounds filled the car, pulling me out of my depression and into the enchanting melody.

The first hint of an idea began to form in my mind. Yet I thought of its dire consequences and what utter willpower it would involve. Could I even pull it off?

I let the music from the radio crowd out my thoughts as we made the short drive to the Landises'. This pact idea was out of the question. Impossible to keep. Besides, just because Abraham had been test-ed that way didn't mean *I* would be.

I found myself sitting high in the hayloft, cuddling two barn cats as I watched Emily and all five of the Landis kids fling themselves out the barn window into mounds of soft hay below. Their squeals of delight kept bringing me back to earth every so often. And I suppose I would've been content to brood there till the first star of evening appeared, but I thought of my sister, knowing I needed to be strong, show some maturity.

So I stood up, brushed myself off, and headed to the open window. Then I did the sensible thing and hurled myself into the air, enduring the butterflies in my stomach as I fell in silent panic into the sweet hay to join the group.

"My mommy bought some surprises for you," the youngest Landis boy informed me as I emerged from the hay mound.

"She did?" I sputtered, regaining my equilibrium.

"Yep, and she's gonna give 'em to you and Emily at supper."

I looked over at my sister, straw clinging to her silky hair. She looked almost like a scarecrow. "That's nice of Aunt Mimi," I said absentmindedly.

The brown-eyed boy nodded his head up and down. "We don't mind having two more sisters round here, honest."

Sisters?

"Well, Emmy and I aren't up for adoption," I told him straight. "Our mother's gonna get well, you'll see."

He didn't bother answering, just scampered off to throw more hay on the rest of the kids.

Everything looked the same as it always did in Aunt Mimi's dining room. Her walnut table was long and opened up the whole way, with one matching bench running along one side of it, mostly for the children. The wide-plank pine floors, the paneling on the doors, and the wide mopboards reminded me of an old-fashioned farmhouse, which, of course, it was.

We'd been told to wash our hands before coming to the table, and it was no wonder, what with all the straw dust on us. I'd taken the time to brush Emily's school skirt off real good—my own, too—before ever entering the screened-in back porch. Made me almost wish we were allowed to wear overalls like the Landis boys.

Anyway, this was a safe, loving place. The people who lived in this house served the Lord and honored His Word. They also loved to sing in four-part harmony. After the table blessing, they broke out in a song, and I thought of Mommy in the hospital, singing praises to God in spite of her pain. And I wished something would happen to make her well again.

My soul was sick with panic; my throat ached with sorrow. So much so that when Emmy and the Landis kids began to sing along, I tried to hum but nothing came out.

After supper, Aunt Mimi's two older daughters and I cleared the table and washed and dried the dishes without any assistance. We made quick work of the kitchen while Emily and the boys played Parcheesi on the living room floor.

I was deep in gloomy thought, staring at a wooden market basket filled with dried Queen Anne's lace and other wild flowers, when Aunt Mimi came into the dining room. She was carrying two wrapped presents with bows made of yarn. "Emily, come see what I bought for you and your sister."

Emmy didn't have to be called twice. She came bounding over to have a look. "Oh, pretty," she said, eyes wide. "How come?"

Aunt Mimi's face grew pensive. "No reason, really. Just wanted to do something nice, since your Momma's sick."

Emily unwrapped hers first. I cringed as she ripped off the green tissue paper and yellow bow, eager, as always, to get to the best part.

"Oh, it's just what I needed!" She held up the pink plastic case to house her many paper dolls.

"It's perfect," I said.

"It sure is. Thank you!" Emily threw her arms around Aunt Mimi's neck, then turned and focused her eyes on the remaining present. "Becky's turn," she said.

I was careful not to tear too much of the paper or break the bow. Emily, and now the Landis girls, were gathered around, watching. Made me a little uncomfortable, being hovered over like that.

The lid came off easily enough, and I lifted out an Amish doll, complete with long black apron and head covering. "She's darling," I whispered, noting the peculiar lack of facial features.

"I found her at Central Market, downtown. Might be fun to play with her, just like you would a regular doll," said Aunt Mimi. "But mostly, I thought you could talk to her...sometimes."

"Maybe so." I studied the blank face now, remembering that Amish folk don't believe in "making any graven images," which included photographs, drawings of themselves, or sewing eyes, noses, or mouths on their dolls.

When I turned to thank Aunt Mimi, I realized that Emily and the other girls had left the room. "I guess I was thinking too hard just then," I admitted. "Where'd everybody go?"

"Out back," she said. "The car has a sprung sprizzle. Mel and the kids are all out there looking under the hood."

I wasn't sure what a "sprung sprizzle" was exactly, but it sounded like something was busted, probably bad enough to allow time for a heart-to-heart talk with Aunt Mimi.

"Thanks for such a nice gift," I said. "Lately, I've been doing too much worrying...talking to myself, too." I told her how the boy on the way to the bus stop had teased me for it. "Guess I oughta try to pull myself together."

"Aw, now, Becky." She led me into the living room where she sat down and patted the sofa cushion beside her. "Ain't all that good to be worryin' so, love. Maybe when you feel the fear a-comin', you could talk to your faceless Amish doll instead. It'd almost be like talking to the Lord, 'cause, after all, He's listenin' in all the time anyway."

I glanced down at the doll in my lap. Maybe Aunt Mimi was right. Looking at the handmade gift, I realized the benefits of talking to something that couldn't see you, couldn't stare a hole right into your heart. "She can't talk back, either," I said, and we both laughed about that.

When I played my Schubert piece for Aunt Mimi, I felt right at home on her old upright piano. Seemed to me not many people could afford much else in the way of a nice instrument these days.

As I played the stormy section, I thought of Mommy, wondering how she was feeling tonight, and then I did a strange thing. I imagined a battle going on between her good cells and her bad ones.

Tears welled up, making my hands appear to swim over the ivories, and I was thankful that Miriam Landis had gone to look out the front window.

Long after the final chord died away, my fingers lay on the milk-white keys, stroking the soft ivories, worn from years of use. I gazed lovingly at the old instrument and my young "piano hands," as Mommy often referred to them.

The good cells *had* to win out.

I kept staring down at the keys, and as I did, something began to settle in my mind. Maybe the idea I'd had earlier *was* possible. With God's help, I could do anything. The Bible said so.

Trembling, I realized what such a promise to the Almighty would mean: my greatest sacrifice. And I'd do it, too, in order to get His attention. Surely, then, the Lord would heal Mommy.

Chapter 10

On Sunday morning, Daddy came and picked us up for church. We could've gone to the Mennonite meetinghouse down the road with the Landis family, but Daddy wanted us with him.

I was glad, too, because I couldn't picture myself going forward to a church altar other than my own to present myself to God. Today was the day, even more critical because of Daddy's words to us in the car.

"People will be asking about your mother." He drove till we came to open road and pastureland on either side. Something was on his mind, because after he pulled into the parking area, he turned off the ignition and looked at us without speaking.

"What's wrong, Daddy?" I asked softly.

He shook his head, holding on to the steering wheel with both hands. "I wish Mommy could come to a healing service" was all he said.

"Can she leave the hospital?" Emily asked.

"Not in her weakened condition," he said. "It's

out of the question."

So she *was* worse.

"Why not take the service to her?" I suggested.

Daddy looked at me, somewhat startled. "How do you mean?"

"Take the elders and deacons and anoint her with oil."

He nodded. It was a wonderful idea. And we walked into church holding hands. Three trusting souls.

The sermon was based on the fifth chapter of Job. I'd heard it preached before, but not by Daddy.

"'But if it were I, I would appeal to God; I would lay my cause before him,'" my father quoted.

I underlined the Scripture in red ink, staring at the words. The verse was doing something—giving me an even stronger, more determined spirit. But the best part was yet to come. Verse nine: "He performs wonders that cannot be fathomed, miracles that cannot be counted."

Scarcely able to sit still, I waited for the sermon to end, for the last hymn to begin. My shyness seemed to disappear as Brother Harris offered the benediction. Folding my hands, I closed my eyes in reverence.

I would appeal to God; I would lay my cause before Him....

Over and over, the verse whispered to my heart.

Lee Anne stayed at the altar and prayed with me for a while before going back to the nursery to help with her baby brother. I needed privacy and scanned the area, making sure no one was within earshot.

He performs wonders...miracles that cannot be counted....

Jittery with anticipation, I began to pray at last. "Dear Lord Jesus, *You* know the end from the beginning. You know what I have on my mind and in my heart. So please hear this humble prayer from me, Becky, one of Your faithful children."

I forged ahead, uncertain of my confidence. "I feel it is Your will for me to offer the music gift You have given me...."

Pausing, I bit my lip.

"I offer it in exchange for Mommy's healing. This means that I'll give up playing the piano forever—all the days of my life—if You'll take my mother's cancer away."

I sighed. "Starting today, I am placing my musical talent on the altar of sacrifice—just like Abraham did with Isaac. In Jesus' name I pray. Amen."

I hadn't realized I was crying until I opened my eyes and saw the evidence. Quickly, I found a tissue in my pocket and wiped the altar rail dry.

A tide of joy washed over me, and I rose to my feet and went to find Emily.

On the way home, we stopped off at the hospital, waiting in the parking lot for Daddy to run inside and visit with Mommy briefly. I looked up at the third story, trying to decide which room was the sunroom. One of these days, Daddy had promised, we'd catch a glimpse of Mommy at the window.

In the backseat of the car, Emily played with her new paper doll case, arranging and rearranging the clothes and hats and accessories, mumbling to herself.

I turned around and watched for a while before she ever noticed.

"Wanna play?" she asked.

"Paper dolls aren't for tweenagers."

She frowned. "You're not a tweener or whatever—not yet."

"I'll be thirteen next April," I reminded her.

"So what'll you do with your Amish baby doll then?"

"I'll give it to you."

"Oh no, you won't," she retorted. "I don't like that doll."

"How come? I think she's unique."

Emily positioned a long, beautiful gown on her paper doll, holding it in place as her fingers pressed the tabs down on each shoulder, then under each arm. "She's got no soul, that's why."

"Because there's nothing on her face?"

"The eyes are the windows to our souls, aren't they?" she asked. "Isn't that why Mommy's are so pretty?"

No arguments from me about our mother's aqua blue eyes. "I guess I could sew on some eyes," I offered.

"Good idea."

"Might spoil her looks."

"No...do it right away," Emily insisted.

"Won't be today; we don't sew on Sundays."

"Tomorrow, then, after you practice for Winter Festival."

The conversation came to a sudden end as I contemplated what I would tell Mrs. Patterson come Tuesday. Of course, I wouldn't go into a lengthy explanation about dropping out, nothing like that. But I'd have to be leaving her piano studio for good, that was certain.

Even harder would be giving up the coveted pianist position for the Christmas Ensemble. I took a deep breath, pondering the situation.

Monday after school, I sorted through our classical records, looking for Tchaikovsky's *1812 Overture*.

Deliberately keeping my back to the piano—to avoid seeing the beloved instrument—I placed the record on the turntable. Then, because the house was empty except for Emily and me, I turned the volume way up. Lofty, triumphant music filled the living room.

"I love this piece," I shouted over the thunderous orchestra. "We're studying it at school, in music class."

Emily agreed, "playing" the cello as I directed her.

When it came to the section featuring the exploding cannons and repetitious descending scales, I pretended to conduct the entire orchestra, waving my arms gleefully to the beat. "There's something about Tchaikovsky," I told her. "He grabs you and won't let you go till the very end."

"I know what you mean."

"His music stirs my soul," I admitted.

She laughed with me, bowing rambunctiously on her imaginary cello. I was still playing conductor as the music moved toward the boisterous finale.

"Which do you like better—your Schubert *Impromptu* or this piece?" she asked.

I caught my breath but kept going. Having done my absolute best to divert my attention from this specific hour after school—the hour I had always devoted to piano practice—I was peeved that Emily had brought up the *Impromptu*.

"Well, which is it?" she persisted.

I let my arms fall to my sides and stared at her. "Is it really possible to have a favorite piece or composer?"

"*I* think so."

"Who's your favorite?" I asked, turning the tables.

"Chopin is nice. Especially the waltzes," she said. "They're so romantic."

"You're too young to be thinking such things." Nervously, I waited for her to mention Schubert again. Then without warning, she got up and headed to our bedroom.

I didn't pursue her but carefully placed the recording back in its jacket and hurried past the piano, refusing to look at it.

Emily had sensed something amiss. I was fairly certain of it.

On Tuesday I called Mrs. Patterson during school lunch hour. The halls were noisy, but this was my only chance to break the news to her before my scheduled lesson time. I didn't want to be rude and cancel too late in the day.

She answered on the second ring. "Hello, Becky. How are you?"

"Fine, thanks." What I had to say must be said quickly; otherwise, it might be impossible to say at all. "I...uh wanted to tell you that I won't be taking piano anymore."

An awkward silence followed. Then—"Well, I must say that I don't understand. Is there a problem we should discuss?"

"No...nothing like that," I answered. "I've enjoyed studying with you very much."

"Well, I guess I don't know what to say."

"Are you wondering about Winter Festival?" I asked, bringing up the ticklish subject.

"After all your hard work—my goodness, how splendidly you were performing the Schubert...."

"I'm very sorry to disappoint you, Mrs. Patterson, really, I am. I was looking forward to this competition, too. And I hope you know how much I appreciate the help you've given me all these months."

She offered to refund my audition fee, but I declined. It wasn't her fault I was quitting.

That night, she called and talked to Daddy. He was as shocked to hear the news from her as she had been hearing it from me.

"How can this be?" Daddy asked, sitting down with me after the long phone call. "I thought you were doing well with this new teacher."

I nodded, praying silently for wisdom. "She's very good, really. It's not Mrs. Patterson's fault."

He removed his glasses and wiped his eyes with a handkerchief, though I knew he was puzzled, nothing more. "I'm concerned about what this news may do to your mother," he remarked.

"W-what do you mean?"

"It will come as a surprise to her, as you must know. Certainly, it would be unfortunate for her to suffer unduly over your quitting. You know how much she loves to hear you play."

Mommy...suffer because of me?

Daddy put his hand on his forehead. "Why would you want to give up the piano, Becky? You're so very talented. I don't understand this sudden decision."

"I adore playing the piano," I said. "But I love

Mommy more." That was all I could say.

"But, honey..."

"I, uh, I can't talk about it, Daddy. Really, I can't."

He seemed confused and distraught, and it pained me to think that my decision had affected him so.

Sighing audibly, he said, "Perhaps, if you're entirely sure about this, Becky, we should wait and break it to Mommy after her treatments are finished."

I hadn't thought about that. "When?"

"Sometime in February."

Such a long time.

I wondered, too, what I could possibly say if she asked me to play the *Impromptu* over the phone again. But I dismissed the distressing thought. "How soon can Mommy come home?"

"Her doctor hasn't said. Could be another week, at least."

I was upset to hear that, but I was glad about *one* thing: My father had not pressured me for the real reason behind my decision to give up piano. Had I told him too much?

The true test of my resolve—and willpower— was yet to come.

Chapter 11

It was Emily who had the courage to be nosy and ask. She was setting the supper table while I experimented with a simple but tasty rice casserole I'd learned in Home Ec.

She came right out with it. "Why'd you stop taking piano?"

There was no straight answer other than the truth. But I couldn't tell my sister about my treaty with God. Chances were, she wouldn't understand.

"Did you quit because of the money?" she asked.

I turned around. "What're you talking about?"

"It must be costing Daddy a lot to have Mommy in the hospital so long."

Two weeks and one day....

I could've nodded or mumbled, giving assent, but it would've been a lie. I wouldn't deceive my sister, or anybody else, about the pure and holy thing between the Lord and me.

Emily was staring at me now, waiting for an answer. I was caught between that rock and a hard place I'd heard some visiting preachers describe in sermons. "I don't want to talk about it, okay?" I said as humbly as I could muster.

She shrugged her shoulders and turned to the task at hand. "Hope Daddy makes it home in time to eat with us before prayer meeting."

I agreed. Our father's visits to the hospital were beginning to extend into the supper hour. "Let's ask to go along tomorrow night," I suggested.

"We'll do our homework in the hospital lobby." Emily came over and watched me chop pickles. "Maybe we won't feel so far away from Mommy that way."

I shouldn't have been surprised when I noticed her lower lip quivering. "Aw, Emmy, I know how you feel...honest, I do."

We held each other there in the kitchen—me, wearing Mommy's ruffled gingham apron; Emily, crying her eyes out.

Wednesday, October 1

Dear Diary,

I had no idea how hard it would be to give up the piano. It was naïve of me to think the first day would be the hardest and that eventually the urge to play would just go away.

To be truthful, the desire grows stronger

*with each twenty-four hours that pass, and
tonight is only the end of the third full day.*

*I prayed longer than usual at church,
reminding Jesus of Mommy's need for
healing. Something else, too. I prayed for
strength to carry out my end of the bargain.*

*My choral director must've thought I
was nuts today when I told him I wouldn't
be playing for the Christmas Ensemble. He
didn't make such a fuss about it, really, but
I knew by the look on his face that he was
shocked.*

*Mary Beth Peters was thrilled, though.
(She's one of the other accompanists—the
next best after me.) It was all I could do to
stand there after class while she hugged me
and thanked me for "this wonderful oppor-
tunity."*

*Oh, to think that I must never play
again....*

"What's Joanna gonna say about you quitting
piano?" Emily said on Thursday.

We were waiting for the school bus, standing by
ourselves as the other kids hung back. They sent
frightened glances our way, and I found myself feeling sorry for them. Too bad someone couldn't let
them know that cancer could *not* be transferred to
them through us. Yet I didn't want to cause a scene,

and I believed it wouldn't be long before we could announce that Mommy was cured.

"Joanna will be very surprised, probably," I replied.

"No kidding!" Emily shot back.

"Look, I can't worry about *everything*, can I?"

She arched her eyebrows. "You usually do."

"Well, this morning I have a history test to think about. I'll talk to Joanna when I see her."

"Better get ready, 'cause that'll be this Friday," she volunteered. "We're going to Aunt Audrey's for the weekend."

Another weekend away from home. Would I ever adjust to the uncertainty, being shuffled from place to place? I didn't blame Daddy, not at all. Besides, Aunt Audrey and Uncle Jack's home was actually a very comforting alternative. Not that Aunt Mimi wasn't kind and so very thoughtful of my sister and me. But it went much deeper with Aunt Audrey. We were, after all, her sister's children, and we knew she loved us dearly.

How our auntie could sing the old hymns from memory. Sometimes she recited the lyrics to us without singing—like poetry. I knew it took some doing because I'd once tried saying all four verses of "The Solid Rock," and failed.

Thinking of Aunt Audrey, I was happy that we were to spend the weekend there. She might have some insight into Mommy's progress. And Joanna, her daughter, was my closest cousin, so there'd be no time wasted in superficial pleasantries. My cousin and I were close in age and went way back to toddlerhood. We had been blessed with mothers who appreciated good music, so we'd grown up loving some of the same things. It just might be a fun time after all.

I came close to spilling my secret that weekend. Joanna and I had already brushed our teeth and dressed for bed when I told her how homesick I was for my mother.

"I wish you could visit her," she sympathized.

For an instant I was struck with the sin of envy. *Her* mother was strong, a model of good health. "I'd like to sneak into the elevator when nobody's looking," I confessed.

Her eyes were wide. "You wouldn't really do that, would you?"

"Getting caught would be worth it if I could see Mommy again."

She covered her mouth with her hand, probably horrified that I was thinking such wicked thoughts. But I needed understanding, wanted her to help bear my burden.

Intentionally, I slid away, perching myself on the edge of her big bed. My bare feet dangled over the side, and I felt the tickle of the embroidered bed skirt as I pouted.

"I'm sorry, Becky," she whispered, tugging on the back of my pajama top. "It's not easy for any of us. I love your mother, too."

It was then that my eyes fell on a small ceramic statuette of a grand piano, white and shiny, atop Joanna's dresser. My contract with God and all its implications threatened to burst forth.

Instead of telling her what I'd done at the altar last Sunday, I began to cry. For the first time since the science class incident, I let hot tears roll down my cheeks, unchecked.

"Mommy, something's wrong with Becky," I heard Joanna calling.

Aunt Audrey hurried into the bedroom. "Dear, dear girlie, what is it?"

I buried my face in my hands, sobbing.

Joanna tried to explain. "I think it's about missing her mother."

"Well, of course she does." Aunt Audrey sat beside me, patting my back. "Why don't we talk to Jesus about this?"

I began blubbering unintelligible sounds, but Aunt Audrey prayed anyway. When she finished, I blew my nose and, in general, tried to calm down. But it wasn't easy with that beautiful miniature piano right in my line of vision.

Soon, my aunt was tucking both of us in, kissing our foreheads. Before she left the room, I asked her to tell me about Mommy. "Is she getting any better?"

"The radiation makes her very tired. But that's part of it."

"Is it working? Is it killing off the bad cells?"

She cradled my hand in both of hers and was silent for a moment. "I saw your mother again today. She's trusting Jesus for her healing."

"Did she tell you about the verses God gave her?"

"Yes, and now there are even more," she replied, stroking my hand. "Your mother wants to live to see you and your sister grow up."

"I want that, too. More than anything."

"But not more than you want God's perfect will performed in your mother's life."

The words stung my heart. Had I tried to alter God's will by forcing my own? Had I been too selfish, wanting my own way? Was *that* why I'd made the pact?

"Now, Becky," she was saying, "the very best thing you can do is to fully trust the Lord Jesus for your mother's safekeeping...as I am."

It was Aunt Audrey's gentle way that soothed me most. I wondered then if sometime, in years to come, I might want to tell her about my deal with God. Joanna, too.

From that night on, I determined to lean harder on God's will, but that didn't mean I was going back on my word. I'd made a promise I intended to keep.

The Lord knew I meant business, even before our church pianist took sick on Saturday, and Daddy asked *me* to play for the Sunday song service.

Chapter 12

I was packing up my Amish doll, along with my pajamas and other things, when the phone rang Sunday morning.

Uncle Jack picked up the receiver in the hallway, then called to me. "Becky, it's your father."

Rushing to the phone, I said, "Hi, Daddy. How's Mommy?"

"I'm going to need your help, honey." He sounded a bit edgy, ignoring my inquiry. "Sister Stauffer is sick with a cold. I know it's short notice, but will you fill in for her during the morning service?"

I couldn't believe it. Why was God letting this happen?

"There'll be the usual three or four songs from the hymnal," he was saying. "Don't worry about an offertory this time."

"Uh...wait, Daddy. I...I can't—"

"What is it, honey?"

"I'm sorry, but I can't do it."

"You've always been so good at sight-reading

hymns. I thought—"

"It's not the practicing, Daddy. I'm just not...not playing piano anymore."

He was in a hurry to leave so he could come pick us up. "We'll talk more about this." His voice sounded stern, almost provoked.

How could I tell him I wasn't being disobedient at all? How, without confessing what I'd done?

At church, Daddy led me into the ushers' room, a small, soundproof cubicle just off the foyer. The place had no window, but there were built-in cupboards where purple velvet offering bags were stored, as well as tithe envelopes and missionary pledge cards. Extra folding chairs, too.

He asked me to sit down and I did. "I don't mean to pry, Becky, but your disinterest in the piano concerns me." He sighed. "Does it have something to do with Mommy?"

The question took me by surprise. Had the Lord revealed the secret alliance to my father? Is that what Daddy was trying to say?

I hung my head, bearing both humility and near defeat. What if I obeyed him—went ahead and played for the congregational singing? And then...what if Mommy died? Forever and always, I'd regret not telling Daddy the truth so that he'd understand and wouldn't force me to play.

Lifting my head, I looked at him. "I guess I

should tell you why I can't play. It's about..."

My heart was throbbing; my breathing irregular—coming too rapidly.

I would appeal to God.... The Scripture trumpeted in my brain. Dizziness blurred my vision as I attempted to speak.

I would lay my cause before Him....

The room began to spin. "Oh, Daddy, I feel funny, I..."

He dropped to his knees in front of me. "Becky, you're terribly pale!"

Then down...down I slumped. Daddy's hands were pushing my head between my knees, gently applying pressure to the back of my neck. He was saying my name, intermingled with the Lord's, over and over.

I don't remember much else, except that Lee Anne and her mother came in and stayed with me through most of the song service. It was the one and only time our church folk had ever sounded like Mennonites. They sang beautifully, without any kind of musical accompaniment at all.

"You never sewed eyes on your doll," Emily reminded me that evening.

"I'm getting used to her the way she is," I said, scrubbing the kitchen counter.

"Well, maybe if you hold up some buttons for the eyes, that'll give you an idea of how she'd look."

"True." But I was dragging my feet on purpose.

She left the kitchen, returning in a few seconds. "Where does Mommy keep the button jar?"

"Same place as always."

She shook her head. "It's not there. You better go look."

I tossed the dishrag to her. "Finish wiping the countertops."

I hurried upstairs to the linen closet in the hallway across from Emily's and my bedroom. We'd stayed home from evening church because Daddy was concerned about me. I could've told him why I was suffering and spared him the anxiety. Honestly, though, I was thankful that the Lord had put a fainting spell on me that morning.

As for resting most of the day, that was the norm for Sundays, at least at our house. Daddy was often exhausted from his duties: teaching the Men's Bible Class during Sunday school, followed by an hour or so of preaching.

Mommy liked to nap on Sunday afternoons, too. First, she and Emily and I would work together in the kitchen: Mommy, putting away the leftovers; Emily, clearing the table; and I, washing dishes. Emily and Mommy would dry them, trying to keep up with me. All the while we sang or chattered about the morning service and the dear folk there whom we loved.

Sometimes—and these were the best Sundays of all—Lee Anne's mother or the wife of one of the deacons would invite us to have dinner with them.

Sharing food, or, as Daddy called it, breaking bread with your brothers and sisters in Christ, made the food taste even better. Fellowship was a big aspect of our church family at Glad Tidings.

In the summer, we'd spread quilts or sheets out on the grass and have picnics after church. Then, if there were people itching to be baptized, we'd turn the social gathering into a spiritual one.

Daddy and another man, usually Lee Anne's father, would wade out into the creek near the church, muddy or not. There, the newest members of the kingdom of God always came up from their water baptism either shouting or weeping.

Afterward, Daddy and the others would change into the dry clothes they borrowed from the secondhand clothes in the missionary barrels. Later, after a trip to the parsonage, those same garments were returned and sent overseas, the smell of creek water and soil completely vanished, thanks to Mommy's box of Tide and our trusty clothesline.

"Find some buttons yet?" Emily's voice startled me from my reverie.

"Uh...just a minute," I said over my shoulder.

Rummaging through Mommy's linen closet was always lots of fun. You could find sheets and pillowcases—sometimes matching, sometimes not—and blankets, a few more threadbare than others. Bath towels, washcloths, and an occasional fingertip towel or hand towel, too. But high on the top shelf, the most unlikely things often appeared if you were looking hard enough. Things like jars of old buttons.

Some as old as the hills, or at least Mommy said so.

Her collection wasn't representative of mere odds and ends. Many of the buttons told a story. There were buttons from long-ago jumpers worn during grade school by Mommy and her sisters. Buttons from special-occasion frocks and suits, because in those days—Emily and I called them the "olden days"—people wore their clothes till they wore out. They didn't let anything go to waste, including the buttons left on tattered garments.

All of Mommy's button jars were organized by color, which meant that one jar held only white, cream, and yellow buttons. Another stored only pinks and reds.

Standing on tiptoe, I reached for the blue and purple buttons. Thinking of Aunt Mimi's gift, I wondered how blue button eyes might look on my faceless doll.

"What do you think?" I asked Emily, holding two small buttons up to the doll.

She tilted her head, looking intently. "Too big."

I searched for a set of smaller buttons, mismatched, but blue nevertheless. "How's this?"

She stepped back, studying the face. "I think the Amish know what they're doing."

"Huh?"

She shrugged her shoulders, coming back to have a closer look. "The doll looks better *without* eyes."

"Know what I think?" I said. "I think she listens better because she's blind."

Emily twisted her long locks. "Is that why you talk to her so much...late at night?"

Flabbergasted, I stared at her. "Why, you've been playing possum, Emily Owens!"

She grinned, mocking me. "She can't really hear you, ya know. You oughta talk to God instead."

"I do, probably more than you."

"Do not."

"Do so."

This was hopeless. I wished I'd gone to church with Daddy.

Chapter 13

Monday, October 6

Dear Diary,

I'm staring at the elevator doors at the far end of the hospital lobby. Emily and I wanted to come along with Daddy tonight. Guess we're tired of being lonely.

Anyway, we're here, doing homework and not talking to strangers, but the hours drag on and I'm worried we'll be droopy-eyed for school tomorrow.

Mommy's just two floors above us, somewhere in a semi-private room. I've never asked Daddy what it looks like, but I'm pretty sure I can imagine how it smells. Down this hallway and around the corner, there's a drinking fountain, and the scent of the place starts to change if you get too close to the nurses' station. It's a lot like rubbing alcohol or something stronger, maybe.

I'm so worn out, I could lie down on this sofa and go to sleep. Sure wish those elevator doors would open up and spill Daddy out!

"What did Joanna say about you quitting piano?" Emily asked, looking up from her book.

"Please, Emmy, not now, okay?"

"Well, *when*?"

I shook my head. "It's too complicated."

"And I'm not old enough to understand, right?"

I groaned; couldn't go into it, just couldn't. Why wouldn't she just leave it be?

"So...what's complicated?"

I glanced at the clock. "Let's phone Mommy's room, okay?"

"You're ignoring me," she whined, closing her book.

I found some change in my wallet and headed over to the receptionist's desk. Timidly, I asked for my mother's phone number. "She's in room 317."

"Would you like to use this phone?" the lady offered.

I looked down the hall, toward the telephone stalls. Craving privacy, I told her, "I'll think I'll use the pay phone...but thank you."

She nodded, wearing a quizzical expression.

When the phone rang, Daddy answered.

"Uh, hi...it's Emmy and me. Are you about ready to go home? I mean...it's getting kind of late."

I heard him exhale, then pause for a moment. "That's right...you're downstairs, aren't you?"

"Did you forget?" I glanced at Emily who was making a sour face.

He was saying something to Mommy now, and because the voices sounded muffled, I knew he'd covered the phone.

Daddy had forgotten, all right. I waited, trying to sort out the situation. Poor, dear Daddy—a quiet, reserved man—was caught up in a swirling storm, with Mommy at its center. *Any* father might have forgotten given the same dire circumstances.

He was back on the line in no time, apologizing repeatedly. "I'll be right down, Becky," he said. "Two minutes, okay?"

"If it's all right...uh, could I talk to Mommy?"

"She's feeling a bit drowsy, but I'll put her on."

I waited, longing to hear her voice again.

"Hello, honey. Are you and Emily all right?" Her voice sounded weak. Husky too.

"We're just tired, that's all."

"Daddy's so sorry...he has a lot on his mind."

"I know. We're fine," I assured her.

"Is your homework finished?" she asked.

"Yes. Emmy's too."

"Wonderful. And your school grades?"

"Okay, I guess." Emily's were better than mine.

Mommy stopped talking, and I didn't know if I

should say something or wait for her to speak again.

At last she said, "Oh, honey, it's so hard to think of my precious girls being right here in this very building, yet too far away to see...or to hug."

"I know. I hate it, too." Then I got brave. "How much longer, Mommy? How long before the doctors let you come home?"

"Well, that's being decided tomorrow," she said, her voice sounding lighter. "Maybe they'll release me sometime this week."

"Really? This week?" I *had* to tell Emily. "Just a minute."

I told my sister the news. She grabbed the phone. "Mommy! You're coming home?" she burst out.

I watched my sister's eyes dance with anticipation, and though I didn't realize it at first, I began to breathe more steadily. Even the knot in my stomach was easing up.

The pact was paying off!

I didn't even notice Daddy step off the elevator, I was so excited. He came over and stood next to me, waiting for Emily to say good-bye.

"Give me a hug," he said, wrapping his arms around both of us. "What kind of father forgets his little girls?"

"You're the best father ever, Daddy," Emily said as we headed for the door.

"The *very* best," I echoed.

"Tomorrow, we'll come again. And you'll get to see Mommy," he told us. "She'll go to the sunroom and wave from the window."

If only I could see the sunroom for myself. What a beautiful place it must be! I could just picture Mommy there. Reclining on pillows propped against a wicker chaise lounge. Soaking up life-giving rays of sunlight...breathing in air freshened by the many lush plants around her. Growing stronger each day till she was able to stand, unassisted, and wave vigorously to Emmy and me. "Come, my darlings! Take me home!" she would say. "God has answered our prayers!"

"Goody!" Emily said, breaking my train of thought.

I was just as thrilled as my sister but responded the way a young lady might. "It'll be wonderful to see her."

"What should we wear?" Emily asked, tugging on Daddy's coat sleeve all the way out to the car.

"Whatever you like, honey."

I had a great idea. "Let's wear our matching dresses." We had mother-daughter dresses but hadn't worn them for weeks—not since Mommy's illness.

"We could bring our gifts from Aunt Mimi and show Mommy...from the parking lot," Emily suggested.

"Yes...let's!" I said.

"Then it's settled." Daddy opened the car door and we climbed in. But he wasn't as jovial as he might've been—about us seeing Mommy. I hoped he wasn't discouraged over having forgotten us. Knowing Daddy, he probably was.

I made sure that Emily was asleep long before I whispered my prayers that night. The faceless doll lay next to me on the pillow, and as strange as it seemed, I delighted in having her near. She was comforting to me in much the same way as Mommy's button jars, her bed pillow, and the matching dresses she'd made for my sister and me.

In that moment of reflection, I knew what was attracting me to the doll. She had become a substitute for Mommy's listening ear. Aunt Mimi had chosen well.

"Pst! Emmy, are you awake?" Didn't hurt to double-check.

I waited, listening for a giggle...anything.

Good. It was safe to talk out loud to God, not to the doll, even though my sister had become thoroughly confused about it. Thank goodness I'd never mentioned the pact in my bedtime prayers.

I was desperate to unlock my soul to my heavenly Father. He'd created me with music in my fingers and in my heart, then had prompted me to give it all up, and now I *needed* Him to help fill the void, the gnawing ache inside me. Because not playing the piano was starting to make me sick. Not sick like Mommy's cancer or Sister Stauffer's bad cold, but sick in spirit, I suppose.

A big part of me was missing. And the longer I went without making music, the worse I felt.

"Dear Lord, I don't have to keep reminding You, but eight days have passed since I last played the piano. Can you help me find something else that brings as much joy? Something that will help me express myself—the real me—again? I'm Your faithful girl. Amen."

The prayer sounded hollow...selfish, too, as I lay thinking it. I stared at the night sky, missing Mommy and yearning to see her face through the sunroom window.

"Tomorrow," I whispered, holding the Amish doll up to listen to the stars. "Tomorrow's the day."

Chapter 14

Never had the hours of a day stretched out so long.

My homeroom teacher had gotten wind of the standoffish cliques in the 7-Y section. She also took me aside and said she was sorry to hear that my mother was ill.

"No student should have to suffer like this at school." Her eyes were soft as doves. "I'm going to put a stop to it."

It was a lovely thing she was attempting to do, but unless she knew how to handle the catty girls who'd started all the morbid talk... Well, the whole thing seemed rather hopeless to me. Still, I appreciated her interest and told her so.

"You're welcome to talk to me anytime, Becky. I'm here for you, okay?"

"Thank you," I said. Too bad she hadn't thought to take out an ad in the school paper. Maybe that would convince the entire seventh grade that Becky Owens was *not* the plague!

It was late afternoon when we pulled into the hospital parking lot. Shadows and light played off the trees and parked cars interchangeably, and I was the first one to squint up at the third floor of the building.

"Which window?" I asked.

"There." Daddy pointed. "See those in the corner? Now, count past two more, to the left."

I wondered why we hadn't brought binoculars. Trying to find an obscure figure in the window this far away wasn't my idea of "seeing Mommy" at all.

The smell of burning leaves was thick in the air, and geese flew in a straight V formation overhead. It bothered me that a siren rang out in the distance, penetrating the stillness and my concentration.

"Does she know we're here?" I asked, fidgeting.

Daddy didn't bother to check his watch. He kept his eyes fixed on the floor above.

And then...there she was, standing at the window, a nurse on either side of her.

"See her?" Daddy nearly shouted.

Emily jumped up and down. Next thing I knew, my sister was perched on Daddy's shoulders, waving with both hands. "Does Mommy see us?"

"I'm sure she does," Daddy replied.

I wasn't quite as excited as my sister, I guess. Maybe because Mommy looked painfully thin, even in her terry cloth bathrobe. I worried as I saw her lift her hand and wave to us...and smile. She just looked so frail, moving her hand back and forth. Like a china doll—one that you didn't dare touch, only kept out of reach on a high shelf to admire from time to time.

She was gone from view as quickly as she'd come, so quickly that we completely forgot to hold up the gifts from Aunt Mimi to show her.

Emily was bemoaning the fact, but I had a great idea. "Take my Amish doll up to Mommy when you visit her," I told Daddy as he opened the car door. "That'll put a smile on her face."

Emily didn't mind entrusting her paper doll holder to Daddy's safekeeping. "Tell Mommy she can look inside if she wants to," my sister said, relinquishing the cherished pink plastic box.

"Consider it done," Daddy said, and we followed him into the hospital for another session in the waiting room.

It was as Daddy punched the elevator button that I thought of letting Mommy borrow my doll— "to keep her company till she comes home."

Daddy nodded. "Are you sure?"

"I'll get her back pretty soon, won't I?"

The elevator door opened. "We should know something tonight," he promised, stepping on.

"I'm praying."

He threw me a kiss.

Am I always praying? I wondered as I headed back to Emily. The Bible said to pray without ceasing. Did that mean in your subconscious, too?

Last night I'd awakened myself mumbling. I discovered that I was talking in my sleep—to God—and I knew it for sure, because I remembered the last sentence: "Please, Lord, heal Mommy."

Emily and I were sharing the loveseat closest to the elevator when out of the blue she said, "I hate recess."

"Don't say 'hate.'"

"Well, I *do*." And she told me how miserable she was at school. "Are you sure cancer isn't catching?"

"If it was, everybody at church would have it by now. And what about Daddy? *He* doesn't have it, and he sees Mommy every single day."

"How can you be so sure he doesn't? He might...it might not be showing up." She looked terribly innocent. Her hair, nearly flaxen, was caught back in a long, wavy ponytail, and those brown eyes, so serious, too direct.

"Trust me, Emmy, you can't catch it."

She wrinkled her dainty nose. "Tell that to Janice and Velma."

I closed my book and turned to face her. "You want Daddy to talk to your teacher? I'm sure he will."

I filled her in on what was happening at the junior high level. "If you have a teacher rooting for you, it'll make all the difference. At least, that's what I'm counting on."

Beverly Lewis

She was silent for a moment. Then—"Is that why you quit piano? Because the choir kids were afraid you'd give them cancer?"

"That's ridiculous." I shook my head in disgust. Her middle name should never have been Christine, I decided. "Nosy" fit her much better!

Chapter 15

Wednesday, October 8

Dear Diary,

Mommy's coming home tomorrow, but it's not such good news, I fear. Daddy doesn't know it, but Lee Anne overheard him telling her father that the doctors have done everything they can. They're sending Mommy home to die.

I think part of me is dying, too.

Where are you, God?

After prayer meeting, Daddy and the elders of the church went to the hospital to anoint Mommy with oil and to pray.

Aunt Audrey went out of her way to drive Emily and me home. She stayed just long enough to see us inside, and afterward, I went around checking the locks on all the doors.

The cats followed me from room to room, acting a bit apprehensive. Maybe they were picking it up from me. To say that I felt uneasy was an understatement. But I never let on to Emily.

Before Daddy arrived home, I'd gathered up two loads of laundry and tucked my sister in bed. That done, I was hoping for a private talk with him. I knew I shouldn't stay up too late, but it would be impossible to fall asleep until I heard his key turn in the lock.

So I prayed while I waited. Knelt right in front of the piano, leaning on the bench, and talked to God. "It's me again, Lord. I'm sure You remember what You and I agreed on."

I couldn't say anything about the pact out loud, not with Emmy in the bedroom at the top of the stairs, this side of dreamland. I sighed, opening my eyes. The old piano seemed to tower over me, like a tall and menacing soldier.

Quickly, I went back to prayer. "Not everyone gets an earthly healing miracle. I know that. Lots of times You cure people another way—a miraculous but hard way, especially for the loved ones left behind."

I had to stop for a moment, refusing to cry. This prayer was too important to let emotion choke out my thoughts. The Lord and I needed to work things out.

Getting up, I tiptoed up the steps and peered into the dark bedroom. Relieved that Emily was asleep, I closed the door.

Back at my prayer post, I continued. "I've been thinking about the song service tonight. Grandpa beat the rhythm with his hands and asked us to 'raise the roof,' but I couldn't sing much at all because of the lump in my throat. How come everyone else at church can praise You even though Mommy's so sick?"

I heard Daddy's Chevy chugging into the driveway. "Well, I better say 'Amen' now, Lord. Remember, I'm Your faithful girl. Amen."

I didn't have the heart to ask Daddy for some one-on-one time. He looked drained, ready to collapse. "Thanks for helping out tonight," he said, removing his coat. "Is your sister asleep?"

"Yes, and the clothes are in the spin cycle."

"You're a wonderful girl." He came over and hugged me. "Mommy sends her love. She'll see you tomorrow."

"I'm counting the hours," I said, thinking maybe it was a mistake for her to leave the hospital. Where doctors and nurses could monitor her condition. Where they might keep her from dying....

Daddy headed off to bed, and I went downstairs to put the damp clothes in the dryer. While I waited, I read half of the book of Job. It gave me a whole new perspective on the trials of my life.

Still, I worried, fearful of what was to come.

Chapter 16

Mommy had already arrived home from the hospital when Emily and I came in from school, eager for our grand reunion.

Daddy supervised our hugs and kisses, making sure we were gentle. And we were, but nothing could keep us too far from her.

We ran to get more pillows, plumping them up on the sofa where she reclined, smiling, obviously happy to be home.

Eager to be with her, to gaze on her face, to see if she looked as pale and frail as I'd remembered, I pulled the rocking chair over next to the sofa. "I thought you'd never come home," I said.

"Seemed like forever," Emily agreed.

"Well, we're all together again," Daddy said. "And God is good."

Mommy didn't say much, but her eyes sparkled occasionally, not reflecting vim and vigor, but gladness. She returned the faceless doll and thanked me for loaning her such a good "friend."

Aunt Audrey came over just before supper with several frozen casserole dinners to stock the freezer and one enormous hot dish, ready to go. She didn't stay long, but she greeted Mommy and gave me a reassuring hug just before she left.

I followed her outside. "Thank you," I said. "You're the best auntie around."

"Don't worry now, Becky," she said in my ear as we hugged. "Give your mother to Jesus, no matter what."

I nodded, watching as she headed out to the car. She meant well, I knew that. But I couldn't honestly say that her parting words helped much. Jesus and I had something else planned. Something very different.

Mommy was too weak to come to the table, so we took a tray in to her in the living room, where she sat on the sofa.

"I may not be able to eat much," she said, eyeing the beef and noodles.

Awkwardly, the three of us stood there, as if doing so might assist her in readjusting.

Daddy spoke up, "If there's anything you need, we'll be just around the corner."

It bothered me that she was still separated from us at mealtime. I don't think I said one word as we ate, so deep was my pain—my feelings of helplessness.

Worse, Mommy asked me to play my piece for Fall Festival after supper—the Schubert

Impromptu she loved. Emily observed closely, waiting to hear what I'd say.

Instead of going to the piano, I went and sat on the floor next to the sofa. "I'd rather be close to you" was all I could manage.

Emily looked my way. So did Daddy. "She's being weird about the piano," my sister told on me.

"Now, Emmy," rebuked Mommy. "Things will get back to normal, in time."

I cringed. *Time's running out....*

Daddy opened the Bible, diverting our attention to God's Word, away from the potentially volatile subject at hand.

I scarcely heard the devotional, enjoying the sweetness of having Mommy near. Reaching over, I held her hand, leaning my head on her arm as I sat cross-legged on the floor. I felt sick that I couldn't fill up the air with the music Mommy loved. Couldn't bring her a few precious moments of joy.

Goldie and Angie made a beeline for me, fussing over who might end up in my lap. Angie won out, but I pulled Goldie over and made room for her, too.

After school the next day, Mommy asked again. "It's been so long since I've heard you play, honey."

My heart ached with the refusal. I was caught between a pact and my dying mother. What could I do? How could I explain what I'd done—was *still* doing—to try to save her?

Once again, Daddy intervened as Emily smirked. And I knew I couldn't go on this way. Something had to give.

Daddy devoted himself to caring for Mommy day and night, and it seemed he thrilled to the task, though it took its toll on him after several weeks. The burden became almost too heavy for him, and I saw it in the way he walked and the way his eyes lost their sparkle.

My mother was patient and gracious, not one to complain. But there came a time when she began to require round-the-clock assistance. So Aunt Audrey, Aunt Mimi, and several ladies from the church—though they each had families of their own—divided the daylight hours into thirds and began sharing the responsibility.

I, on the other hand, felt useless. Nearly every day Mommy would ask me to play the piano for her. Having to repeat that I simply couldn't do it was ripping me in two. What was I doing to her? To myself?

One night I overheard her and Daddy talking. "Does Becky seem stubborn to you...about her music?" she asked.

I stood in the hallway, leaning against the wall, almost wishing it would cave in and crumple me into the floor.

The most haunting words came next. Daddy told her that my heart was broken. "I honestly think Becky's so worried that she *can't* play anymore." He paused for a moment. "She loves you that much, dear."

I inched forward, listening for Mommy's reply. She gave a tired little sigh. "Becky must learn to trust. Can you help her with that for me?"

There was an overwhelming stillness. I could only imagine what was taking place in the solitude of their room. But I was sure that Mommy was comforting my father in her own lovely way, sick or not.

Indian summer faded all too quickly. Soon, November was upon us, with its beguiling smells of cinnamon candles, eucalyptus wreaths, and a turkey-flavored Thanksgiving.

December followed close behind with the promise of Christmas. *Holy days*, Daddy liked to say, and this year, more than any other, I referred to the holidays that way, too.

The school Christmas Ensemble concert turned out okay, I guess, considering the painful circumstances. Instead of playing the piano, I sang, which was light years removed from being "the" accompanist for the group.

Several times during the first song, Mary Beth caught my eye. I knew she was trying her best to figure out why *I* was singing alto up on the second riser while *she* sat center stage at the piano, instead of the other way around.

Christmas Eve was like every other night before Christmas I remembered from age seven or eight. I curled up in the only overstuffed chair we owned, wrapped up in one of Mommy's afghans. The vocal score of Handel's *Messiah* in hand, I turned on the old radio, ready for two hours of heaven.

Mommy lay on the sofa, dozing in and out, determined to join me in our annual tradition. "I can hardly remember a Christmas when we skipped Handel," I said.

"Mm-m. It's going to be beautiful." Her voice was growing softer these days, as if fading. Her energy level was more down than up. I wondered about her will to live. Was Mommy giving in to the cancer?

I'd kept track of the days—now weeks and months—since I'd played those final piano chords at Aunt Mimi's. Three days shy of three months.

Though there were times I felt as if I might shrivel up and die without my music, I was learning to compensate. *Listening* to music had taken the edge off the harrowing experience. That, and thinking I might teach piano someday. Might attempt to pass on my love for the instrument to young children, though I had not determined how I could do so without actually performing for them.

So the pact was ongoing, and I continued to exercise my faith in hope of a miracle, though the discordant reality became more evident with each day that passed.

As for Mommy's requests for my playing, she seemed to have forgotten—almost as though she were concentrating now on her own concerns. Perhaps a divine focusing on things to come. The hereafter; heaven, in particular.

While the *Overture* began, slow and majestic, she recounted her Bible college days for me, though I'd heard the story many times. How she had enjoyed presenting *Messiah* with the choral group there, singing two solos—"Come Unto Him" and "Rejoice, O Daughter of Zion."

I listened attentively, both to the music and to Mommy, getting up only to light several more candles to heighten the enchantment of this sacred evening.

The Christmas tree, how it glistened, surrounded by the most glorious music this side of the pearly gates. Emily and Daddy wandered in and out of the room on their way to the kitchen, making popcorn and hot cocoa for themselves and me, and tall glasses of carrot juice for Mommy. But for the most part, the musical ritual of this magical night belonged to my mother and me.

Occasionally, she hummed, and I joined in, too, being careful not to cover her wispy voice with my youthful, strong one.

She talked of the sunroom, how light and airy it had been. "Oh, I wish you could've seen it, Becky. So brilliant and warm, with streams of sunlight to bask in."

Why she'd think of the hospital on a night like this, I had no idea, but she was indeed caught up in a passion for the place. The lovely room, no doubt,

had offered her a respite from the cancerous storm.

"Like the Holy City, God's heaven must surely be," she said almost in a whisper. "I'd hold the phone close to my ear, listening as you played the piano here at home. Oh, Becky, hearing your music made all the difference."

"It did?" I asked, hesitant to pursue it.

"You'll never know how much it helped. I imagined you sitting at the console piano in the corner of the sunroom, your fingers flowing over the keys...."

Hard as I tried, I couldn't recall her mentioning a piano in the sunroom.

Her face was radiant now with the remembrance. As the opening strains of the "Hallelujah" chorus began, she turned to me suddenly, stretching out her hand. "Oh, honey, play this one. Play it along with the radio."

"Mommy, I—"

"Please, Becky. I want to hear it...want to *feel* it."

I looked at her lying there, so ravaged by pain. Was she slipping into heaven even as I sat here, sharing our beloved music? Was Jesus calling her home on the night before His birthday?

Something urged me on. No longer could I refuse her. I had the power to give her the very thing she longed for—that thing she desired to bring her joy, to lessen her physical agony.

But if it were I, I would appeal to God....

Mommy was appealing to me, her Becky, her firstborn—the little girl she'd encouraged to play the piano all those years ago. That faithful child of

God who had been given the gift of music.

Pushing the afghan aside, I went to the old upright piano. If Mommy was going to die, why not obey her, do what I could to ease her across the golden shore?

I sat down, my hands poised on the ivory keys. Silently, I prayed. *Dear Lord, please understand what I must do....*

Chapter 17

The New Year made its debut, blowing more snow and cold around than December ever dared to. Eagerly, I began writing in a brand-new diary—a Christmas present from my parents.

After thinking about it for some time, I decided to write a dedication on the first page, something I felt prompted to do. Not so much out of shame for having broken my end of the pact or trying to get on God's good side again—nothing like that. I did it because I believed that my heavenly Father, the supremely divine Parent, had forgiven me. Had overlooked my blundering, childish mistake, because He knew my heart better than I knew it myself.

Almost a teenager now, I was growing wiser in the Lord. By consuming the Scriptures, as Mommy had, I was learning to trust God's plan for her future. And for mine.

So I penned these words on the first page:

The Sunroom

This diary is written to the glory of God.

January 1

Dear Diary,

*I'm playing the piano again—prac-
ticing more than ever (up to nearly two
hours a day and improving, I must say).*

*I've learned that God is the giver of
every good and perfect gift—my musical
talent, for one. I've learned the hard way,
I guess. The hardest way!*

March came all too quickly. She fooled us with
an early thaw, then dumped an ice storm on all of
Lancaster County. Spring was out of reach, yet
Mommy hung on to life's rough sea, buoyed by
hours of my piano playing each day. She had taken
to her bed just after the New Year, and Aunt Mimi,
as well as Aunt Audrey and others, had continued
to assist with housework and cooking. And tending
to Emily and me.

I joyfully resumed my piano study with Mrs.
Patterson, at Daddy's request. My teacher gave me
some new music for the spring Sonatina Festival,
but Mommy asked me to keep playing the
Impromptu.

The kids at school were kinder, more accepting
of me as the weeks turned toward spring, passing

the six months mark—that bleak forecast for the duration of Mommy's life.

In late March Daddy took on a part-time job to help pay the hospital bills, working for a tree nursery in addition to his regular pastoral duties. All the while, Aunt Audrey reminded me not to worry.

But I *did* worry. Every day, every single day, I hurried home from the bus stop to see if Mommy was still alive.

The road from the top of the hill to the end of our lane grew longer and longer. Where was spring? If Mommy could make it past spring—maybe to Mother's Day—she might fool the doctors and live, I decided.

I looked for signs of crocuses pushing through the snow along the road. In the neighbor's yard, I searched for buds on the pussy willow bush. Each afternoon, I watched the sun slant its rays against our fence, the shadows inching farther toward the road like bony fingers.

Upon arriving home, I would lean hard on the back door, out of breath. Then shoving it open, I'd race up the stairs. *Mommy!* I couldn't call out, could only breathe the words. *Are you still here? Are you alive?*

Then, one mid-April afternoon, I found the shades drawn, probably to soothe her eyes. When I peeked in, the room seemed drearier than usual. Daddy had moved the dresser and mirror, positioning the bed at an angle so my mother wouldn't have to see her own sallow face or her thinning hair.

I took off my shoes and left them in the hallway, then crept across the room. Softly, I began to hum the melody from the *Impromptu*.

She opened one eye. "You're home."

I knelt beside her bed. "It's my birthday."

Turning her head, she smiled. "I know. Happy thirteenth."

"Spring is coming. It *really* is," I whispered. "I saw my first robin."

"Was it singing?"

"No, but he looked chipper enough to."

That made her smile again. "What piece are you going to play for me today?"

"What would you like?"

"Something exciting," she said. "You pick."

The *1812 Overture* came to mind. "I know the perfect piece—only it's not for piano."

"Help me sit up, will you?" There was a hint of a twinkle in her eye. "I can hear the music better that way."

I found her bathrobe, then moved several more pillows to support her back. "How's that?"

She looked at me, studying me. "Something's different about you, honey."

How could she possibly know?

"You've become a young lady, haven't you?" Her eyes, as blue as asters, saw right through me.

I nodded, feeling the warmth in my cheeks. "Right before Valentine's Day."

"Bless your heart, sweetie."

We laughed together. I turned to go, embarrassed. "Ready for some noisy music?"

"How about a little sunshine first." She motioned toward the drapes. "Please?"

Wasting no time, I pulled on the cords at the far end of the windows. There on the eaves stood a beautiful bird sporting a plump red vest. "Look! That's my robin!"

"Oh...help me out of bed, Becky. I want to see him up close."

Steadying her as she leaned on my arm, I peered out, amazed at this moment.

"It *is* the first robin, isn't it?" she whispered as we watched.

"The very first."

Startled by my voice, the bird flew away.

"Quick, play the music," she said. "I want something rousing."

I helped her back to bed, noticing a hint of color in her face, then scurried off to find Tchaikovsky. "It'll grip you from the start," I shouted up the stairs.

"Play away," she called back, and if I wasn't mistaken, there was a merry ring to her voice.

Her jovial mood lasted only a few days, then Mommy took a turn for the worse. I worried that she had experienced something akin to the energy surge the body puts out just before a person slips away. I'd heard enough about it, what with the many elderly relatives on Mommy's side.

And there was Grandma. The same thing had happened before she died. We thought she was getting better, going to be healed. And she *was* healed. Her ailing body just fell asleep and woke up completely well in a place called heaven.

I recorded my thoughts:

Sunday, May 3

Dear Diary,

Mommy returned to the hospital today—one week before Mother's Day. Daddy missed out on preaching his sermon, and Emily and I went to eat Sunday dinner with Uncle Mel and Aunt Mimi after church.

I can't explain it, but having Mommy leave us is harder this time, and the toughest part is Emily's reaction. She's a little older now. Maybe that's it; I don't know. But she clings to me all the time and keeps asking a million questions. Mostly about dying and how hard it is to walk through the "valley of the shadow of death."

So I'm gentle with her, trying to give her as much attention as a big sister can without mothering her too much—she hates that.

We probably won't be seeing Daddy much this week. Who knows when we'll see Mommy again...on this earth.

Chapter 18

Monday, May 4

Dear Diary,

   We found out that Aunt Mimi does sleep with her glasses on at night. Lies flat on her back and wears them. Must be something like having your heart washed white as snow, ready for the Lord's return.

   Emily found it out first. She got up in the night—was probably sleepwalking— which she does pretty well these days. It's hard to tell if she's awake and walking or just plain dreaming where she's going. Anyway, she walked right into Uncle Mel and Aunt Mimi's bedroom. Scared the livin' daylights out of both of them. Emmy, too, I think.

   That's when Aunt Mimi turned on the table lamp next to her side of the bed.

And there they were—glasses perched on the end of her nose.

You'd think she'd snap them in two, but when Emmy asked her about it this morning at breakfast, she said she never moves in bed. Stays motionless, as quiet as a log floating down the river. I think she meant to say "as still as death," but she didn't, of course.

After school, I practiced my music lesson on Aunt Mimi's piano. It didn't feel or sound much different from ours. I've requested some classically arranged hymns, and my teacher doesn't mind. She thinks it's a good idea, and I'm glad.

"You oughta practice up something for Mommy's funeral," Emily said.

I stopped playing and turned around. "How can you say such a thing?"

"Sorry," she whimpered, backing away.

"Come here." I got up and pulled her over, setting her down on the bench with me. "Don't give up, Emmy. We *can't* give up."

"I'm tired of hoping." It was a whisper.

Thankful that Aunt Mimi or her daughters weren't around, I cupped my hands around my sister's face. "Mommy's not giving up, is she? Just because she had to go to the hospital doesn't mean she's gonna die."

"Seems like it."

"Maybe so, but listen, I want to tell you a story. It's the one Grandma told me a long time ago." I began to tell her about a little girl who was climbing a mountain.

I took a deep breath. "At the foot of the mountain, the breezes were sweet and gentle. The trees and flowers blossomed and grew along the river. Everything was summertime in this valley, and the little girl smiled and kept walking."

"Is she real?" Emily asked.

"Just listen," I shushed her and continued. "The path got a bit steeper, but the girl, who was now becoming a young woman, stopped and caught her breath every so often. She looked out across the glen, enjoying the view in every direction, which made the hard climb worth the effort."

Emily's eyes were wide now. I wasn't sure, but I thought she was catching on.

"The last part of the climb was the hardest. It took every bit of the woman's breath. Her body was older now, so she couldn't just skip up the mountain the way she had in the valley. But she didn't look back at the hollow much, either. No, she kept her eyes on the summit—the highest peak of the mountain."

Emmy was starting to cry. "I don't want to hear the ending," she said. "Please, don't let the lady get to the top."

I thought of Mommy's struggle. How she'd had to learn to live with acute pain. "The sun shone brightly and everything was beautiful at the top of the mountain...like a dazzling room filled with light." I had to stop for a moment. "Like a sunroom."

"Maybe *that's* why Mommy loves the sunroom at the hospital," Emily said.

"She feels close to God there," I whispered.

Emily leaned her head against me as we sat there on the piano bench. "Now you can finish the story."

"Finally the woman reached the end of her long, hard journey."

" 'Cause that's where she dies, right?"

I wrapped my arms around Emily. "We don't know if Mommy's finished climbing. We just don't know."

"But if she is, will Jesus come for her? Will the angels?"

"She won't be alone when it's time to stand on the mountaintop." I remembered the Twenty-third Psalm. "And she won't be afraid, either."

Chapter 19

Daddy wanted to do something special for Mommy on Mother's Day. So did Emily and I. With a little help from Aunt Audrey, who'd invited us over for the weekend, we made cards complete with verses. Actually, Emmy's card had a copied saying in it, but mine was an original poem. One I'd composed especially for the occasion.

Roses are red, violets are blue,
Jesus loves you, and I do, too.
Roses are red, lilies are white,
Happy is she, whose sunroom is bright.

We put colorful stickers on the paper—pretty mayflowers, lilies, and butterflies. They reminded me of spring.

"Mommy has lived way past the doctor's prediction," I told Aunt Audrey.

She was arranging a bouquet of her own, a real one. Stopping to glance at me, she smiled. "Your mother has a strong will to live, and I believe the Lord gave it to her."

"Was she born that way?" Emily piped up.

Aunt Audrey came over to the table where we were working. "What counts is God's grace."

Emily's hair danced as she bobbed her head up and down. "She's not going over the mountain yet," she chanted.

I wondered what Aunt Audrey thought of that, hoping my sister wouldn't blurt out that it was *I* who'd told her a death story. It was, after all, a *life*-and-death story.

"I wish we could take the cards up to Mommy," I said after church. "Along with Aunt Audrey's flowers."

Daddy pulled into the hospital parking lot without a word, and soon we were getting settled on the familiar lobby loveseat. Lonesome for Mommy, I hoped Daddy's visit wouldn't last long.

When he led me over to the elevator, I was confused. He pushed the button. "It was quite an effort, and could possibly be a hospital first, but the nurses have agreed. You're going to spend twenty minutes with your mother on Mother's Day."

"I am?"

He nodded. "Here," he said, handing over the homemade cards and the vase of flowers. "Would you like to deliver these in person?"

I glanced back at my sister. "What about Emmy? Can she come?"

His eyes softened. "'Too young,' they said. I'll stay with your sister."

The elevator doors opened and I stared at them. I'd watched these very doors, listened to their familiar *swoosh*, and wondered what it might feel like to sneak up to see Mommy.

Turning, I thanked Daddy one more time. "This is wonderful. I can't believe it!"

"Hurry, now, before some higher-ups get the notion to change their minds."

I stepped into the elevator. The door closed. "She must be dying," I said to myself. "They're letting me visit my mother for the last time."

The sunroom was even more radiant than Mommy had described it. Large Boston ferns and hanging plants, flowering baskets of blues and pinks, and a darling window seat filled with plenty of pillows. And the light, it poured through the windows like a spray of God's love.

My mother was reclining on the wicker lounge of my imaginings, her back to me. The room itself seemed to reach out and draw me in. Like a soft embrace. And one of the nurses accompanied me inside, making me feel welcome and almost important as I stepped across the tiled floor.

"Happy Mother's Day." I leaned down to kiss

Mommy's soft cheek.

She looked up and deepened her smile. "Oh, Becky, you little dear."

"These are for you." I handed her the home-made cards.

She took her time reading them and looked at me after each one. The nurse put the flowers on the windowsill, and their heads seemed to stand at attention in the warmth of the sun's rays.

"Sit next to me," she said softly.

The nurse pulled up a chair, then left.

I was alone with Mommy at last. "I don't know how you did it, but thank you."

She looked at me, eyebrows raised. "It was Daddy's idea. He wanted us to have this time together."

"How are you feeling?" I ventured.

"Fine...I'm just fine."

I hated it when people said they were fine. You know they're not, and they know it, too.

I tried not to stare, but her stomach seemed so big again, as large as a woman ready to give birth. The way it had been last September.

She crossed her arms underneath like Lee Anne's mother always did when she was expecting.

Not knowing where to look, except for her face, I bit my lip. She eased the situation, inquiring about school. One of her favorite topics, as always.

So we discussed seventh grade. "It's almost over," I said. "I'll be in eighth next fall"—as if she didn't know.

"You've grown up so much, just since Christmas. I wonder how tall you'll be." Her mind's eye seemed to struggle with this glimpse into the future.

"I think my biggest growth spurt is over. Look at my feet," I pointed out. "Lee Anne says I won't grow much taller because my feet are medium-sized. She oughta know; she's going to be a nurse someday."

"She'll be a good one." Mommy seemed tired. Too tired to pursue this speculative chatter.

"We miss you at home—at church, too," I said. "*Everyone* does." My eyes fell on the small piano in the corner. "Would it be all right if I played something for you?"

"Oh yes," she said, smiling. "Play the Schubert piece, if you like."

I went to the piano and poured my heart into the *Impromptu*, playing the beautiful melody better than I ever remembered having played it all those months before the pact.

When I finished, Mommy was brushing away tears. Her hand reached for mine. "Keep playing, honey," she whispered. "Not only the melancholy tunes. Remember the songs that dance, too."

"I promise." And then I told her everything. Every detail of the pact came spilling out.

"Oh, my dear girl." She covered her eyes with a handkerchief. "God desires only our trust," she whispered.

"It's not easy."

"Trusting comes as you grow up in Jesus." She smiled, blinking back tears.

We were silent too long. It felt eternal. "I don't want you to die."

She didn't turn to look at me. Her gaze was centered on the radiant light pouring through the tall windows. "Death is part of life, Becky. But I won't go till the Lord says it's time." She sighed. "As long as there's life, there's hope."

I chuckled. "You've always said that."

"Yes...."

The sunroom was still, so absolutely peaceful I could've imagined a flutter of angel wings if I'd tried, but there was no imagination required. I was sitting next to Mommy on a splendid, sunny Mother's Day afternoon, coming to terms with truth. With faith.

Give your Mother to Jesus, Aunt Audrey had said. And, silly me, I'd tried to give my music instead.

"I'll love you forever," I said suddenly, as if it might be the last time.

Her face was stained with tears. "My little Becky. You're a sensitive girl...a true musician.

Don't ever let it go."

"Jesus made me this way. He'll take care of me. Don't worry." It may have been a first, me telling *her* not to worry. But she took it with grace, and I leaned down and wrapped my arms around her neck.

We held each other, mother and daughter, without breathing. At least I didn't. Not until I cried and had to let the air out.

Monday, May 11

Dear Diary,

Mommy's having surgery again first thing tomorrow. The doctors are glad our family believes in miracles, because "she's going to need one," they told Daddy.

The surgeon will try to remove the large tumor without taking her life. I'm going to pray all day, even though I'll be at school.

I left my faceless doll sitting on the window seat in the sunroom. I want her there where Mommy can see her first thing, next time the nurses wheel her in. If they do....

Putting my pen down, I reread what I'd written. Then, looking at the clock, I realized it was almost time to wake up Emily. Maybe if I hurried, I could finish this entry....

It seems that time isn't moving forward anymore. It's locked up in a vacuum, and I'm caught in the middle. The feeling is suffocating, and sometimes I don't think I can breathe.

Poor Emmy. I hardly know what to say or do for her. She just doesn't understand why Mommy can't be awake when she takes those last steps up the mountain....

Reflections

The Present

It's odd to think of people reading what I write. Of course, most of them will be family members, people who attend the reunion in July. People like Emily and her husband, Wayne, and their daughters, Bethanne and Bonnie. Uncle Jack, Aunt Audrey, and their children's spouses—and their grandchildren. And my own immediate family, of course.

Grandpa and his second wife have gone on to heaven, but most of my mother's siblings and spouses are still alive.

I heard, too, that the Landis clan may be coming. They're not blood kin but connected, nevertheless. Turns out, one of Aunt Mimi's girls married a Harris boy—Lee Anne's first cousin. And so it goes.

I'm in the dark as to a title for this segment of our family history. Nothing fancy is suitable, for we were never that. Often, we had just enough to go around.

Stepping off a wide circle in the sunroom, I'm surprised at how small it seems. Must come with growing older—climbing the mountain. Entertaining childhood memories of a place causes them to shrink automatically.

Musing further, I notice the plant hooks on the ceiling, trying to remember if any of them were here on that long-ago Mother's Day. "I'll never forget the smile on the nurses' faces," I tell Aunt Audrey, referring to the unexpected visit. "And Mother's, too."

"Whatever happened to the Amish doll?" she asks.

"I gave it to my oldest daughter, and she gave it to *her* firstborn, along with the story behind it," I explain.

She nods, then turns toward the footsteps in the hall, moving aside to give me full view, past an old piano and through the doorway.

There, leaning on Daddy's arm, comes my dear mother, slowly making her way to the sunroom. "Happy birthday, Rebekah," she calls gaily.

"I couldn't keep her away," Daddy offers, with a loving glance at his petite wife. "Not when she heard you were conducting research here at the hospital. This occasion would not be complete without your mother, you know."

Daddy's clear gaze searches mine in a moment of sweet communion, and my heart is full of love and appreciation for this quiet, gentle man.

"How'd you find me?" I ask, suspecting Aunt Audrey, whose mischievous grin gives her away. "I should've known."

We round up some folding chairs for my parents, and Mother reaches for my hand. "How's the writing coming?"

I feel self-conscious. "Enlightening, at best."

"Good...good. I'm anxious to read about myself," she says, chuckling.

"You're the miracle girl," I say.

Daddy and Aunt Audrey are nodding quite emphatically. "The Lord gets top billing," he says, raising his right hand in acknowledgment to heaven.

After a time, Mother gets up and goes to the window, looking down at the parking lot. "Just think, after all these years, I'm still free of cancer," I hear her say. Then she whispers, "'He performs wonders that cannot be fathomed, miracles that cannot be counted.'"

My heart catches in my throat. So God has linked us once again—all those awful days of waiting so long ago. My eyes fill with quick tears, my heart rejoicing in His unfailing goodness and love.

My mother turns suddenly, the light playing on her graying hair. "How about some music?" she says to me.

I'm nearly giggling. Me, a grown woman, losing it in front of my aging parents and one incredible auntie. "What would you like to hear?"

"Oh, the *Impromptu*, by all means."

I sit down, playing with as much or more emotion than ever, struck with the realization that time has become a physician, healing the past. *My* past.

The room is drenched in ribbons of gold as the sun slips over leafy trees and quaint row houses far below. And the music fills the spaces of our lives, of